BURIED IN YOUR ABSENCE

CORINNA C. ROY

Buried in Your Absence
Corinna C. Roy

Book Formattig and Design by Rachel McEwan

Edited by Brittni Van

ISBN 979-8-218-87012-6 (paperback)

ISBN 979-8-9941255-1-9 (ebook)

Published by Corinna C. Roy

www.authorcorinnacroy.com

For every fat, horny, infertile woman out there. I see you; I am you.
This one is for us.

AUTHOR'S NOTE

This story is a healing fantasy. A love letter to the parts of myself I've struggled to embrace. As a woman navigating infertility, I've often felt like my worth was measured by what my body could or could not do. Omegaverse, with all its messy, emotional, and deeply intimate dynamics, became a place where I could escape, imagine, and reframe those fears through fantasy.

In the Omegaverse, people possess secondary genders—Alpha, Beta, and Omega. They influence instinct, biology, and social dynamics. Heats, ruts, mating bonds, scent recognition, and knotting are common traits in this subgenre. It's a world often rooted in longing, vulnerability, and raw connection. But more than that, it's a world where I was able to pretend that my body would do what I wanted it to do.

Writing this reminded me that womanhood isn't defined by a uterus or a diagnosis. It's found in resilience. In softness and fire. In all the beautiful, valid ways we show up in the world.

So, if you are tall, short, fat, skinny, trans or otherwise, I hope this story holds space for you, too.

With love,

Corinna

CHAPTER 1
ROSIE

Lazy, quiet mornings in bed are the closest thing to heaven. That first long stretch as you drift awake, still tangled in sheets and the scent of your mate—

Mate.

I stretch my arm out, reaching for the familiar mass of muscle that usually fills the other side of the bed. Instead, my hand finds only a heap of blankets, already growing cold.

I always feel a little unmoored when he's gone too long. Like my body forgets how to settle without his warmth tucked in behind me. These long jobs pull him away for days, even weeks at a time; and even when I know he'll come back, this state of yearning is damn near impossible to keep at bay.

Theron works wilderness security assignments, guarding remote lodges or research sites where the cold bites and predators stalk the shadows. It suits him, even if it leaves me lonely in a bed that only ever feels too small when he's in it, and far too empty when he's not.

Without Theron, my desire to stay curled up in bed all day vanishes. Instead, I have the need for something, anything, to occupy my mind. To make the time away from him go as quickly as possible.

I crawl my way out of bed tugging the covers off and wrestling the fitted sheet into submission before fluffing the pillows and smoothing out the wrinkles in our floral-patterned duvet. Then I start tackling the mountain of laundry I've been conveniently ignoring for the last couple days. It's my least favorite chore but it has to be done.

I press my nose to each shirt, inhaling deep, imaging my tall dark-haired Alpha. His green eyes half-lidded, voice thick with longing. I separate the ones that still hold his scent, setting them aside in a not so neat pile for my nest.

My nest.

It's my little corner of the world, built for comfort when everything else feels overwhelming. When my heat hits—or when I just miss him too damn much—I curl up in it. Blankets, pillows, soft shirts that still carry his scent. *Theron.* His smell grounds me. It eases the ache, soothes the loneliness, and reminds me that even when he's gone, I'm still his.

I pause halfway through folding one of Theron's hoodies, frowning with confusion as I catch myself tucking it aside with the others, building a now sizable pile of dirty clothes thick in his scent, like I'm on autopilot.

"Nesting." The word rings loud in my mind. I stare down at the lump of clothes I've gathered, shirts and shorts of his.

The thought prickles the back of my mind. I'm not in heat, not yet at least. So why does every part of me want to burrow, and be surrounded by his scent?

Maybe it's the emptiness he left behind that's doing this. His absence a constant reminder of my nature to always be close to him. It's already been a few days, and it doesn't get easier with time. If anything, it gets harder. Like my instincts are screaming for something my brain knows I can't have.

And yet, I'm just paranoid enough to check my calendar.

I always track my cycles, more because of Theron's insistence than my own desire to plan every damn heat.

We have been trying to conceive for what feels like forever, but we've had very little luck. Most would say no luck at all. And it's become a sore topic to say the least.

Theron keeps urging me to track every detail, like it'll help. Like watching it closer will somehow make the stars align. But hopelessness has already taken root inside me, and I fear it just won't be possible for us, no matter how much planning we do.

I count the days. From my last heat in November to now. *February.* From now to when the next one *should* start in March.

I read it once. Then twice.

I even check the little notches Theron helped mark on the wall calendar, just to be sure.

And, oh God.

I fucked up.

My heat isn't early, it's right on freaking time.

Panic coils hot and fast in my chest. I've never dealt with a heat alone. Not since we bonded, and that was years ago.

I feel a little foolish, honestly. I'm not incapable. Heats are natural. I'll be fine. I'll just need to prepare before it really burns. Because when it hits, it's like my blood turns molten and every nerve ending is tuned to ache.

My body will lust for touch. I'll sweat through the sheets, thighs slick and trembling, mouth dry from panting. I won't be able to think about anything else. Just the overwhelming need to be filled. That's heat.

It's not simple lust. But biology cracking through willpower.

"Take your time, Rose. One step at a time," I reassure myself and start making a mental list.

Water. Food. My favorites of Theron's clothes… God, I wish he were here instead of needing to cling to scraps to curb my need for him.

I should secure the windows, double check the locks. An Omega in heat is vulnerable, and the last thing I need is some stray Alpha sniffing around where they shouldn't.

And the vibrator, the one I had custom-molded after Theron's cock, definitely needs to be charged. It's not the same, never will be, but in the thick of it, sometimes it's the only thing that helps take the edge off.

It's a short list, but it feels like a mountain of work.

The thought of doing this without Theron is making me panic. I don't know when the impossible-to-ignore sensation will hit. Could be hours, maybe longer… maybe sooner.

But the not knowing? That's what makes everything feel so urgent. Like I'm racing a clock I can't see.

I start with water. I tuck three bottles under my arm, another clutched to my chest as I make my way back to the bedroom and set them on the bedside table.

I gather my pile of Theron-scented laundry and toss the clothes onto the bed, some landing in a messy heap, others crumpling into the corners like they're already waiting to be burrowed into.

Then I dig through the kitchen pantry, searching for the stash of granola bars Theron always keeps hidden for me.

"Just in case." he'd say, brushing my hair back with that crooked little smile of his. "Never know when you'll need them, Rosie."

I hate it when he's right. Which is all the damn time.

I double-check the locks on every door before finally retreating to the bedroom. It's a safety measure I've never had to think twice about since living here. But given the fact I'm all alone, I can never be too careful.

Being an Omega means carrying a constant, quiet caution. We're seen as the fairer sex. More delicate, more vulnerable. Our bodies are meant to bear children and submit to instinct.

And while the world has come a long way, some dangers still linger.

An Omega in heat emits a scent that can turn even the most controlled Alpha feral. Most are respectful. Most know better.

But "most" doesn't mean all. And I've heard too many horror stories to take chances.

Theron's presence and pheromones are usually enough to keep any wandering Alphas, and even a few bold Betas, from sniffing around where they shouldn't.

But not this time.

This time, I don't have my Alpha to guard me. I have to think about protecting myself.

And maybe that's what really sets me on edge—because I haven't had to think about my safety in so long. Not since the day we married.

No… even further back than that. Not since the day we met.

From the moment Theron stepped into my life, I've felt protected in a way I never had before. Like his presence alone formed a barrier between me and everything that ever made me flinch. He became my shield. And I haven't felt afraid since.

It was a bar. One of those trendy rooftop places my friends had dragged me to after work. Too many bodies, too many pheromones in the air, and more Alphas than I was comfortable being around.

I remember trying to be polite when a pair of them cornered me by the bathrooms. I'd smiled, said I wasn't interested, and tried to walk away ending their delusions quickly.

That should've been the end of it. But , of course, it wasn't.

The moment I rejected them, their attention turned cruel. One of them sneered, "Fat girls are always easy," while the other called me "ripe," like I was something to paw at, like I should've been grateful for the attention.

I've always been curvy. Soft hips, thick thighs, a belly I always try to hide with oversized sweaters. Never thin, never the kind of girl boys fought over. But I was marked early as the 'easy' one. The girl desperate enough to settle.

And because I didn't fold at their advances, they're sweet talking became bitter.

I didn't even have time to panic before he was there.

Theron.

He didn't say a word. Just stepped in between us, towered over them and glared.

One look! That's all it took for them to leave without another word. I don't think they even realized they were backing down until they were already halfway to the stairs.

He didn't look at me at first. Just kept his broad back in front of me like a living wall, his shoulders tense beneath the stretch of a worn leather jacket.

His body radiated heat; the kind that made you forget the cold ever existed. I remember staring at his back and thinking, nothing could get through him.

I should've been relieved. I should've said my thanks and walked away. But I couldn't move.

Because his scent hit me in that moment. Pine and leather with a sweet undertone. Like a cookie fresh from the oven. Something warm and soft that didn't belong on a man built like a mountain. It invaded every corner of my senses.

He scared me. God, he scared me.

Not because he did anything. Just because of what he was. Huge. Quiet. Dangerous. He'd scared off two cocky Alphas with nothing but his presence, and now he was turning to face me.

His eyes had glowed amber in the low bar lights, his head tilting just slightly, like he was deciding if I was worth the effort to speak to.

It was intense. Overwhelming.

And I wanted him so badly, I thought my knees might give out right there.

But I was so consumed with doubt. I was—hell still am—a short, full-figured woman. Nothing like the many available and beautiful Omegas at that bar.

And yet to my utter surprise, he wanted me.

But now I have to try and overcome this heat without him.

CHAPTER 2
ROSIE

Each piece of clothing is placed in just the right way, encircling me. Blankets are piled on top of each other creating the perfect soft bedding. And all of it smells like Theron.

I've never nested in the bedroom.

Instead I've always opted to do so in the library, at least ever since we moved into this house. The room is small, intimate, with custom built shelves filled with all my books. A large lumpy yet incredibly comfortable armchair covered in cozy blankets sits in the corner, and the stuffed animals Theron's bought me over the years rest in a net hovering above it.

But the space wasn't always meant to be used like this.

When we bought the house, it was supposed to be a nursery. But as time passed, that dream started to rot, curling in on itself until it felt like a wound I couldn't stop touching.

Theron, my proud hero, gutted the whole room one day while I was out buying books I had no room for. He turned it into a sanctuary for me, removing the constant reminder of what I still didn't have.

But today, I need our bedroom, that shared space filled with the mixed scent of him and me.

In the middle of our too-small bed, surrounded by fabric and memory, I fuss over each piece like it might be the one that gets me through this.

Heat rolls through my belly in slow, steady waves, dull at first, then sharper, spreading lower until it settles heavy between my thighs.

I shift, pressing my legs together trying to achieve some kind of relief, but it only makes the ache worse. The kind that throbs—constant and unrelenting, like my body's already preparing for him.

My nest should bring comfort. The layers of softness and safety, each piece smelling faintly of him. But it simply isn't enough.

I hold one of his shirts and curl myself around it, breathing in that mix of pine, leather, and sugar. It's a temporary soothing effect, but the need for him is larger. Still, it has to to do for now.

*

In only a few hours, the heat has progressed to make my body and heart ache. My face is flushed, and it feels like the house's AC is off even though I hear it clearly running on overdrive.

The loneliness gnaws at me, deep and hungry, like there's a hollow part inside me that only he can fill. Not with words. Not with presence.

But with his *body*.

His weight pressing me down. His knot locking us together. His voice in my ear telling me I'm doing so well for him.

He always praises me. Always reassures me. Tells me I'm made for him. I was made to be his mate, to bear his babies, to fill his life with sunlight.

"Theron…" I sigh, barely louder than a breath. The heat burns within, growing fiercer. I can feel it stirring beneath my skin like sparks waiting to catch and become a raging blaze.

Being in heat before we were mated was hard, but bearable. It was a slow and long kind of hunger, like a distant itch I had to fight the urge to scratch. But now it's different.

Mated heat doesn't just pull, it demands. It's devastation lying in wait. It's all consuming and quick. Like a flash flood, ripping through me and sweeping me into a current I'll drown in.

In a short time, I'll need him so desperately it will hurt. Thankfully, I'm not at that stage.

But I will be and when this fire finally rages, I don't know how I'm going to survive it without him.

I shift again, restless. My skin feels too warm, like I've been lying in the sun too long. My thighs press together, not out of need but anticipation. The worst part is the anxiety of knowing this is only the beginning.

I close my eyes and try to pretend the nest is enough.

Try to pretend I'm not alone.

And my mind—the traitorous thing that it is—drags me back to that night. The first time my heat hit after we'd started courting.

We'd danced around each other for weeks. Long looks. Soft touches. Him walking me home even when it was out of his way.

I hadn't even meant to tell him. I tried to hide it. But Alphas and their damn instincts, made it futile.

He showed up at my door just after sunset, holding a bag of groceries and a small bottle of suppressants. I don't remember if he bullied his way in or if I invited him. It was probably the latter, honestly. Theron was always careful with me. Never pushed too hard, even when I could see in his eyes how badly he wanted to carve out a place inside me just for him.

I was shaking. Aching. My skin too tight even then, my thighs already damp with need. I remember trying to say no, not because I didn't want him—God knows I did—but because I was scared.

And he just… waited.

Sitting on my couch in my old apartment, like he wasn't a threat, like he didn't fill the entire space, like his scent wasn't already making me dizzy.

I broke first.

Called him into my nest while I laid naked, legs spread and begging for relief.

"Please," I whispered, voice breaking. "I need you. Alpha, please."

And God, the way he touched me.

Slow at first. Reverent. Like I was a gift he didn't know how he'd earned. He stroked my hair, kissed my temple, murmured praise into my skin like every word mattered.

I begged him to claim me, to make his mark and promise. A vow, to bond us forever.

And he did. His teeth pierced my skin. A single moment of searing pain ebbed away with bliss.

He was my Alpha. My mate. My love.

When he finally bit me—when the mark was made—I came so hard I cried.

And he held me through all of it. Never left my side.

The mark aches now, our bond echoing my need. It pulls me away from the memory, I feel as though I just surfaced from underwater. The sheets are twisted around me. My nest a mess. My skin sticky. My breathing uneven.

My heat is picking up speed. Soon, that fire will blaze, and I'll be alone for the worst of it.

Theron

I swipe my phone off the nightstand and stare at the screen, thumb hovering over his contact.

I shouldn't bother him. He's working. But I can't stop shaking. And the urge to cry is getting stronger with each breath.

So, I hit the call button and wait. It rings. Once. Twice. Straight to voicemail.

I close my eyes and begin speaking before I can talk myself out of it.

"Hey, um… I know you're busy, but…" I take a moment to find my words. I don't want him to panic. "I promise I'm okay." I swallow, my throat feeling dry. "I just… I miscounted, and it's starting. My heat, I mean. It's not bad yet, it's just…"

My voice catches. I press a hand to my chest like I can hold the ache there.

"I'm nesting in our room. I know, weird, right? I just—needed to be close to you. It smells like you in here, and I thought that would help, but—"

Another breath. A shaky, embarrassed laugh.

"God, I sound crazy. I'm sorry. I just… I miss you, Theron." My voice breaks again as I say his name. "I miss you so bad it hurts." My throat grows tight with emotion. "You don't have to come home. I mean, unless you can." I sound so desperate, and I quickly try to correct that.

"I'd never ask you to leave a job, I just… I wanted you to know. That it's starting. And I'm being good. I'm being so good." I want his praise, his low voice whispering sweet things in my ear but all I have is this damn phone. "But I'm scared it's gonna get worse before you get back."

Silence for a beat. I sniff. Then I whisper, "Come home, Alpha. Please."

The moment I hang up I'm meant with silence, and I already hate how that message is going to sound when he hears it.

CHAPTER 3
THERON

The wind carries the scent of pine, wet soil, and the faintest trace of something sweet blooming in the underbrush. Tall trees surround me, their vibrant green hues creating a mirage of beauty up toward the hidden sky. This place has the kind of quiet that should calm a man's nerves.

But mine are strung too tight, coiled like wire, just waiting to snap and release me into some kind of madness I won't be able to leash. Beneath my boots, the ground is soft, almost springy with moss, damp from last night's rain. A monarch butterfly floats lazily past my shoulder, its golden wings catching the late afternoon sun like stained glass. I watch it drift, slow and aimless, until it disappears into the trees.

This job is a simple one, at least on paper. It's a security detail to make sure a bunch of field researchers don't do anything stupid while they chase butterflies. There are a few tents. Some solar panels. Gear crates. A dozen bug-obsessed scientists buzzing around with tablets and cameras. All easy to track.

No danger. No threat. No real reason to feel like this.

And yet…

I growl under my breath. I shouldn't be this wound up.

I signed up for the job. Hell, the way my Rosie lit up when I told her about the researchers tracking changes in the monarch migration almost made me care, too.

But at this moment, I just want it to be over.

I shift my stance. My body won't settle. Muscles twitch beneath my jacket. Jaw clenched so tight I can feel the pressure behind my ears.

Something's wrong.

Has been since I woke up this morning. Hell, maybe longer.

The team just thinks I'm grumpy, having a damn mood swing like a bratty teen. One of the interns offered me coffee earlier, called me a bear fresh out of hibernation, and I acted like a class A ass.

I didn't mean to snap at the kid. Barking at him like that was a mistake. I made it up to him—gave him an extra ration this morning and apologized in front of the others.

It helped. A little. At least I hoped it did.

I do another lap around the perimeter just to give my body something to do. The forest is quiet. Still warm from the afternoon sun, with golden light filtering through the trees in soft, dappled patches. There's no scent of predators. No recent tracks. Nothing but birdsong and the occasional drone of insect wings.

Just me. Just the woods.

And still, I can't settle.

I follow a narrow path to the east edge of the camp, not far from where the portable generator hums quietly behind one of the tents. That's when I see it.

A tree, towering and gnarled, covered in a living shimmer of gold. Dozens, maybe hundreds of monarchs cling to its bark. Wings shifting softly with the breeze like the whole tree is breathing.

It stops me in my tracks. Even I have to admit, it's stunning. Like a living picture.

I pull my phone out of my pocket and snap a picture. I don't usually bother, but I know Rosie would lose her mind over this. She'd gasp and call them little bits of sunset. Probably ask if I could catch one for her just to let go, even though she'd tear up the second it flew away.

The thought actually makes my jaw loosen. My shoulders relax.

Maybe that's all this is. Too much time away. Too many nights in a cold cot with no Rosie in my arms.

I miss my girl. *My Omega.*

She's like a drug I'm addicted to, and I'm in desperate need of a fix. A hit. Whatever you want to call it. My system's running low, and I'm going through withdraws.

I glance down at my phone, still in hand. One missed call. One voicemail.

Her name lights up the screen, and I can't help the stupid smile that appears on my face, knowing my girl is thinking of me. It's soft.

I press play, eager to hear her message, but her voice hits me like a freight train.

"Hey, um… I know you're busy, but,"

I go still.

"I'm okay, no need to freak out."

She's trying to sound calm. I can hear it in the rhythm, the fake ease in her voice. But underneath it there's a tremble.

That slight hitch in her breath. The way the last syllable rises just a little too high.

She's not okay.

"I miscounted, and it's starting. My heat, I mean. It's not bad yet, it's just…"

This can't be happening.

She tracks her cycles. Always has. Maybe just to appease my constant nagging, but we track them for a reason. To avoid her being alone when it hits.

Fuck, *I* miscounted.

I should've double-checked the damn calendar. Should've sat her in my lap and counted the fucking days on my fingers if I had to.

Should've trusted my gut this morning instead of brushing it off like a lovesick idiot who just missed his mate.

My pulse roars in my ears.

"I'm nesting in our room. I know, weird, right? I just needed to be close to you. It smells like you in here, and I thought that would help, but—"

My breath stutters.

She's nesting in our room.

The library was always her place, filled with blankets, books, and soft things that made her feel safe. She'd said once that it made the whole thing easier if she kept it separate. Kept the heat separate.

Kept the *ache* separate.

Our room's always been *ours*.

Private. Shared. Balanced.

And now she's there. Alone. In our bed. Curled up in my scent and trying to feel close to me when I'm not there.

Goddamn it, Rosie.

The pride that swells in my chest is thick and hot, tangled with guilt and something close to grief. She's letting herself want me without walls. Letting herself need me. Which means the library—the place I carved out for her when the nursery dream died—*wasn't enough.*

That sacred little sanctuary couldn't hold her this time.

And that tells me more than anything how deep this is hitting her. She didn't want memories. She wanted *me.*

And I left her with a Goddamn voicemail instead.

"God, I sound crazy. I'm sorry. I just… I miss you, Theron. I miss you so bad it hurts."

That last word—*hurts*—comes out like a whimper.

My gut twists.

"You don't have to come home. I mean—unless you can. I'd never ask you to leave a job, I just… I wanted you to know. That it's starting. And I'm being good. I'm being so good."

The message keeps playing, but my mind fractures right there.

God, baby.

My thumb twitches against the phone. My heart burns.

I know you are. Of course you are. Always so fucking good for me. Even now. Even scared and aching and alone, you're trying to follow the rules.

"Good girl," I whisper under my breath like a secret. "My good girl."

She should be in my lap. I should be holding her down, knot buried deep, whispering praise into her skin while she shakes and sobs and rides it out like she was meant to.

Instead—her voice starts to sound thin and distant, like it's traveling through water. Each word barely registers over the roar in my ears, the pulse in my veins.

"But I'm scared it's gonna get worse before you get back."

My entire body locks.

That one word. *Scared.*

My girl, my Omega, is *scared* and trying not to cry, whispering into a phone instead of into my chest.

I fucked up.

"Come home, Alpha. Please."

The message ends.

And for a second, I can't move.

I just stand there in the woods, with the butterflies behind me, and her voice echoing in my ears like a heartbeat that doesn't belong to me anymore.

My mate needs me.

And I'll level mountains if that's what it takes to get home.

CHAPTER 4
THERON

By the time my feet hit the gravel trail back to camp, I'm grabbing for my comm, barking orders I barely remember giving. My brain's gone primal—half instinct, half calculation.

My Rosie needs me.

And nothing else matters.

Not the butterflies. Not the data. Not the paycheck.

Not even the Goddamn lead researcher who steps into my path just as I reach the supply tent.

"Theron! Whoa—hey, what's going on?" Dr. Harbridge's clipboard slaps against her chest as she jogs up to me, brows pinched. "Is there an emergency?"

"Yeah," I growl, brushing past her. "At home."

She follows me. Of course, she fucking does.

"Wait, hang on—you're leaving? Without formal handoff? What

about your shift coverage?"

"I'm not asking permission."

I unzip the tent flap and duck inside, grabbing my rucksack from the corner and yanking open the gear bin. Knife, med pack, spare comm battery, all tossed in without care. My hands are shaking. I can't stop thinking of her in our bed.

Alone. In our room. Breathing out my name into an empty house.

She's writhing, wet, and reaching for me with hands I should be holding down. Saying my name in a voice I should be swallowing.

Another voice pipes up behind me, standing too close.

The second he crosses into the tent, I smell him. Levi. Fresh-showered, overconfident, and absolutely not welcome here.

My scent's all over this place. My bag. My clothes. And now this kid, this child, has the audacity to step inside while my mind is full of Rosie.

Rosie.

Curled up in her nest. Whimpering. Shaking. Begging for me with tear-slicked lips and trembling thighs.

And Levi walks in like this is just another morning briefing.

I'm two seconds from snapping his neck, but I claw together a shred of control and give him one warning.

"Get out. Now." My voice is low, laced with venom and just a semblance of control.

"Sir." He gulps. Clearly, he's scared and yet the little bastard doesn't leave.

Levi puffs his chest, mustering the courage to speak. Another mistake. This kid really is begging me to kick his ass.

"Sir, I understand your urgency, so I propose I take command during your absence. I know the protocols, the shift order, and it helps, I'm one of the few other Alphas under your command." He speaks like he's giving a presentation in some boardroom.

I just keep packing.

The moment I turn around is the moment I know I will lose control. But he's not worth it.

"Levi," I grind out, voice edged with warning, "I'm going to be kind and tell you once more. Leave."

"I just think it would be irresponsible to leave the team without a clear—"

My leash snaps, and I turn with force.

One second he's talking, the next he's airborne. I shove him so hard his boots leave the ground. He hits the dirt just outside the tent with a sharp grunt, skidding into the loose gravel on his back.

A half gasp, half whimper noise that pisses me off escapes him. He was just practically drooling for the top spot, and now, he's whimpering like a fool.

He stays down, arms half-raised like I might finish what I started, head ducked in full submission.

Smart. A bit fucking late, but smart.

I step over the threshold and stand above him, letting him see the difference between him and me.

"Let me make this real simple," I snarl, voice laced with the quiet threat of my anger. "You *never* walk into another Alpha's space without permission."

I lean down, low enough for only him to hear.

"And you *sure as hell* don't walk into *mine*. Not when my Omega needs me."

Levi trembles, nodding without looking up.

"Good," I snap. "Remember that."

I glance up toward the gathering crowd. Of course they heard. Good, they all need this fucking lesson too.

I spot Grant, an older Alpha. He's ex-military, and quiet as hell but sharp. I trust him.

"Grant, you're in command." I bark. "I don't want to hear from this camp unless someone's dead."

Grant just nods once. Doesn't question it. That's why I like him.

I haul my rucksack over my shoulder, walk past Levi without another glance, and growl over my shoulder, "And somebody better clean that shit stain off the floor."

"Wait? Your Omega?" Dr. Harbridge's voice slices through the tension, clipped and exasperated, like she can't believe they're all wasting time over something as inconvenient as an Omega.

I ignore her continuing my stride toward my truck when I hear the whispers.

"Rose? Is she hurt?"

"Maybe it's a heat?"

"Of course. Omegas and their damn heats."

My fingers flex around the strap of my bag. I look down, violent rage bubbling within.

Calm. Stay fucking calm.

I count to three and force a breath out slowly.

I can't lose it here. I know if I so much as look at one of them, I'm not leaving this camp.

I'll be wasting time burying someone in it.

I sling the pack into the truck's cabin and step into the driver's seat of my truck—Rosie's truck, technically, the one she made me drive because she liked the way it looked with my arm hanging out the window.

I can smell her. Like a phantom clinging to my skin. My cock's been half-hard since her message, but now I'm aching. Not just to fuck her but to fill her, to knot her, to make the ache stop.

For both of us.

I slam the door and don't look back.

Not at Levi. Not at Harbridge. Not at the whispering little shits who think a heat is just a nuisance instead of the kind of agony that can shatter an Omega.

They don't deserve an explanation.

They don't deserve her name in their mouths.

"Come home, Alpha. Please."

I turn the key, revving the engine and peel out of the camp, scattering dirt and gravel.

"I'm coming, baby," I whisper, knuckles white as I grip the wheel.

CHAPTER 5
ROSIE

The room burns, like an unbearable summer day. Sweltering heat pierces my skin and leaves me wanting, begging, aching, for cool relief.

My skin itches. My muscles ache. Everything inside me coils and tightens, a pressure I can't escape. It's like being wrung out from the inside. Pain and want tangled together until I can't tell the difference.

I don't know how long I've been like this.

Minutes? Hours? Days?

Time slips through my fingers, and with it, my patience… my sanity. Each minute stretches longer than the last, tangled with heat and desperation, and the more I wait, the more unsteady I feel. Like I'm unraveling by the second.

I only know one thing.

I need him.

"Alpha…"

The word scrapes from my throat, barely above a whisper. My lips are cracked. My body's too hot, burning from the inside out. I twist in the nest, dragging one of his shirts to my chest and sobbing into it like it might answer me.

But, of course, it doesn't.

My body is screaming for his weight. For his knot. For the way he touches me when I fall apart under him, and the world stops hurting for just a little while.

I fumble for the vibrator and nearly sob when it gives a sad, pathetic buzz before dying completely. I must have forgotten to charge it, or maybe I killed the poor thing with overuse.

I reach between my legs with shaking fingers, desperate for something.

Relief. Friction. Anything.

I close my eyes and imagine him above me, knees caging my thighs, his weight settling over mine like a promise. He'd take my wrists, pin them with one hand and cup my face with the other. Call me his good girl while he pushed inside me, thick and slow and deep.

"You're made for me," he'd whisper. *"So fucking perfect like this. Wet and begging."*

I whimper, hips lifting into empty air. The ache intensifies. My fingers aren't enough. They'll never be enough.

My slickness coats my thighs, my fingers, the sheets. It's everywhere. A mess. A flood.

I slide my fingers inside, but it's wrong. Too soft. Too small. My body clenches around the intrusion like it's *begging* for more, but nothing happens. No release. No satisfaction.

Just more need. More *emptiness.*

"Theron," I cry, his name, broken and pitiful. "Please…"

I try to envision the stretch, the burn, the lock of him deep inside me. That sweet, unbearable fullness as his knot swelling and sealing us together while he murmurs, *I've got you, baby.*

My walls flutter around nothing. My body convulses with the need to be claimed, bred, *owned.*

My fingers curl again, deeper this time, but it only makes the ache worse.

Everything I do only makes it worse. Makes the heat burn hotter.

I sob into the nest and yank another pillow against me, humping it like a desperate animal because I *am* a desperate animal now.

I'd let him ruin me if he walked through that door. Beg him to split me open and leave his scent in my lungs and his knot buried so deep I'd feel it for days.

But all I have is this silence. This fire.

And the ghost of his voice in my head telling me to be good.

"I c-can't," I whisper to no one, my whole body shaking. "I can't do this."

The heat crests again, seizing me in its teeth.

And all I can do is cry harder.

I claw at the blankets, at my own skin, curling in and uncoiling like I might be able to outrun the pain of it. But my nest feels wrong all of a sudden. It's too open, too cold. I shove pillows aside and then pull them back in, crying into them like they're him. Like they could hold me down and make the burn stop.

My breath comes faster, ragged and raw.

I'm panicking.

There's too much air, too much space, and not enough of my Alpha.

I whimper, lips trembling. "Alpha… please, I'm scared…"

I choke on the next sob, curling around one of his shirts like it might protect me. Like it might keep the rest of the world out.

I need to be safe.

I need to be *his*.

But he's not here. And I can't do this alone.

What if someone else smells me? Some stray Alpha looking to take what isn't his? I can't protect myself like this.

I've heard the stories—every Omega has. Just weeks ago another one was added to the long list of tales of warning. An Omega was living alone in a studio apartment, and she had to fight off her landlord when her scent turned sweet during a normal conversation. These attacks are… rare but still far too common for comfort.

As Omegas, we're told to lock up. To stay quiet. To hide. Because in this world, even now, a heat isn't just vulnerability. It's a beacon.

The thought makes my stomach twist. I bury deeper into the nest, pressing my body as low as I can, like if I make myself small enough, the danger won't see me.

"Theron," I breathe again, so soft it almost isn't a sound. "Please hurry."

SLAM.

The sound cracks through the air like thunder.

A car door.

Heavy. Final. Familiar.

Everything inside me goes quiet.

The silence that follows is sharp, cut clean by that sound.

That *promise*. That *threat*.

It's either salvation…

Or danger.

And I'm too far gone to tell the difference.

My breath hiccups in my throat.

"Theron…?" I whisper, too weak to cry, too raw to hope.

But still I wait.

Trembling.

Burning.

Begging.

Please let it be him.

Please let him finally be home.

CHAPTER 6
THERON

Eighteen hours. No breaks. Just caffeine and desperation. Most people would've collapsed by now, but Alphas are built for endurance—and I was running on nothing but instinct.

Eighteen miserable, white-knuckled hours racing down winding roads with my Omega's voice echoing in my skull—*"I'm being so good. But I'm scared it's gonna get worse before you get back."*

My poor Rosie.

My beautiful, plump Omega writhing in her nest, thighs soaked in arousal, chest heaving, her heat-induced pheromones filling the entire Goddamn house.

A growl rumbles low in my throat, the weight of my cock pressing hard against my zipper, painful and unrelenting. It's been that way since she called. Since I heard her voice crack. Since she whispered *"Come home, Alpha. Please."*

I drove like a man possessed. Cutting corners, riding too close behind semis, cursing every asshole who dared go the speed limit. And of course, it caught up with me.

The flashing red and blue lights lit up my rearview mirror like a curse. It took everything in me not to tear the door off its hinges and snarl in that cop's face.

But I didn't.

Didn't breathe a word except what was needed. Didn't loosen my grip on the wheel. Didn't let go of the low, warning growl in my chest.

The officer wasn't an idiot. He saw the tension. Felt it. Hell, maybe he even smelled the edge of arousal clinging to my clothes.

He wrote the ticket fast. Gave me a look like he wanted to ask if I was okay, then thought better of it.

He wasn't the enemy. Just doing his job. Too bad it kept me from her that much longer.

Now with a three-hundred dollar ticket, I was only fifteen minutes away from my Rosie.

The engine roars under my hands, but my mind slips back to the first time she let me into her nest.

It wasn't even a full heat. Just the early signs.

That low ache blooming in her belly. The subtle shift in her scent. Sweeter, warmer. Like honey melting on my tongue.

We weren't even mated yet.

Hell, we weren't even *official* by Omega standards. But I was already hers. And she was mine.

She let me into her apartment. It was a small studio, with barely enough room for the two of us, let alone a proper nest.

I remember the way she fidgeted, standing beside that pitiful pile of throw blankets and a couple stuffed animals, trying to pretend it was *enough*.

It wasn't. Not for someone like her. Not for someone who deserved silk and softness and every Goddamn comfort in the world.

She was chewing her lip, avoiding my eyes. "It's small right now," she said. "I have more. I just… I'm a slow nester, I guess."

I didn't hesitate. Honestly, I didn't think about it at all.

I peeled my shirt off and handed it to her.

She stared at it like I'd given her a gift, and like I was fucking nuts. And I was.

Still am.

"If you want me in there," I said, "you can have me. Just say the word."

She took the shirt. Pressed it to her face and inhaled like she needed it to breathe.

Maybe it was the hormones. Maybe it was the early stage of heat making her too honest. But her voice cracked when she said, "I keep waiting for the punchline."

I was stunned. Frozen with disbelief. And simmering anger.

She sat down in her little nest, fidgeting with my shirt in her lap, eyes shiny and uncertain. "You've been so sweet. So good to me. But part of me keeps thinking…"

A breath. A shake of her head. Then the words tumbled out.

"Part of me thinks this is all a setup. That any minute now, you'll walk out and laugh and say 'Just kidding.' Like it's a joke."

I blinked, confused—still a bit naive, maybe, or just blind to the fact that she couldn't see what I did. "Why would you think that?"

"Because I'm not the kind of girl Alphas want to end up with." Her head dropped, her voice small with the weight of her own insecurities.

"What kind of girl do you think you are, Rosie?"

She laughed, bitter and soft "I'm the chunky girl. The one people settle for in the dark, but never bring home to meet their mother. I'm soft in all the wrong places. I'm not adventurous or fun. I'm boring and big and…just not the kind of girl who gets to keep an Alpha like you."

I saw red.

Not at her.

At *every voice in her head* that made her believe that shit.

I knelt in front of her, took her face in my hands and forced her to look at me. "Don't you ever say that again."

She tried to blink away the tears.

"You think I'm pulling a prank?" I growled. "Rosie, if I wanted a toy, I'd have bought one. I want *you*. I want *this*. Nest and all."

She broke like a dam. Tears falling down her flushed cheeks.

She let me pull her into my lap, let herself cry into my shoulder while I wrapped my arms around her and tucked her in tight.

That was the first time I slept in her nest.

There was no fucking. No teasing. No touching meant to arouse. I just held her—in the stillness, in the quiet—and somehow, it was the most intimate thing I'd ever done.

And I'd never felt more needed. More trusted. More whole than when laying in her nest, and her head resting on my chest.

It was the first time she let me have a piece of her softness, without apology, without shame.

I round the last corner into our neighborhood, and that's when it hits me.

Her scent.

Like a bomb dropped straight into my chest.

It rides the wind, thick and unmistakable. Ripe heat. Desperation. That honey-warm pull I'd know anywhere. It's clinging to the trees, perfuming through the vents of my truck, pulling me home like a leash.

I snarl, the sound of a beast about to eat its prey.

My cock jerks against the seam of my pants, throbbing with every beat of my heart. Sweat breaks across my brow, my hands gripping the wheel so tight the leather creaks beneath my fingers.

The overpowering notes of her heat are consuming. Calling me forward. Calling me home.

I turn onto our street like a man possessed, tires chirping as I swing into the driveway. My vision tunnels. The world narrows to that single point of entry.

Our front door, barely thirty feet away.

And behind it? *My mate*…likely tucked into what I assume will be a wrecked nest. Panting, pleading, soaked in everything I've been dreaming of for hours.

I slam the truck into park, chest heaving. My instincts roar, primal and furious, demanding I get to her now. That I put my teeth on her throat and bury myself inside until the world fades.

Mine.

The word echoes loud in my head, over and over like a war drum.

Mine. Mine. Mine.

She's crying for me. Begging. Terrified and alone.

And I'm still out here.

I throw the door open hard enough to shake the truck. Then slam the damn thing closed.

SLAM.

The sound cracks through the quiet street like a gunshot.

My muscles are locked with adrenaline and lust. Her scent is so strong now, it nearly knocks me off my feet. Like a wall of molten sugar and sex, dragging nails down my spine.

My cock throbs, painful and impatient.

My hands shake.

I want her.

No. *I need her.*

The house is twenty feet away. I take the steps in three strides, body thrumming with a tension I can't leash. Not anymore. Not when she's on the other side of that door, slick and soft and sobbing my name like a prayer.

I reach for the handle.

And the only thing holding me back from tearing the door off its hinges is her.

She's scared. Vulnerable. Waiting for her Alpha, her mate. Not a beast.

So, I take a measured breath. Just once. Just enough to steady myself and open the door.

CHAPTER 7
THERON

The door shuts behind me softly, but it might as well be a lock snapping into place.

The musk of her pheromone's hits like a Goddamn wall. Thick and humid, soaked with heat and slick and something else that guts me clean through.

Loneliness. Pain. Fear.

It's all there, braided into the sweetness of her heat. Every twist of her ache written in the air. Like a trail of breadcrumbs meant for me and me alone.

My Rosie.

I move through the house, quiet as I can. Like if I step too heavy, I'll crack the floor open and fall straight into hell.

I pass the bathroom, the open door offers a glimpse of my reflection in the mirror. My jaw is covered in thick, dark stubble. It's short, but well past a five o'clock shadow. I pause for half a breath.

I can only hope she doesn't mind but in the state she's in, she probably won't.

I keep moving, and around every corner I turn, every inch closer I get, the smell sharpens. Thickens. It clings to the walls, to the furniture. To me.

And then I hear her.

Not a voice. Not words.

Just…a sound.

A whimper, fragile and worn. Like it's been torn out of her throat one too many times.

My chest caves in.

She's calling for me and she doesn't even know I'm here yet.

I come to a stop as I stand in the doorway of our bedroom.

And I see her.

God.

She's in the middle of the bed. My bed, our bed. Wrapped in the shredded remains of her nest. Blankets kicked out of place. Pillows stained in sweat. One of my shirts clutched tight to her chest, pressed to her face like it's her lifeline.

Her legs are curled beneath her, thighs glistening with the wet sheen of her arousal. Her skin is flushed, her lips parted, her chest rising and falling in shallow, uneven gasps. Her eyes are glassy, barely open.

She's trembling.

Not from the heat. From fear. And it punches me in the throat.

Because I know that scent. That bitter twist beneath the honeyed ache. She's scared. My girl is *scared*.

And fuck me, it's because I wasn't here.

I was *gone*.

I was hours away while her body begged and broke for me.

Her scent pulls me forward like a leash around my soul. Every note of it slices into me. I smell the yearning, the desperation, the ache to be held, touched, *claimed*. But underneath it, I smell her doubt. Her sadness. The echo of every tear she's cried into the nest I should have been in.

I drop to my knees beside the bed.

I can't speak. Can't breathe.

I just look at her, all flushed and ruined, whimpering like I'm a mirage. Her glassy eyes flicker with doubt, unsure if what she's seeing is another dream…or her mate finally coming home.

She shifts, just barely, and another broken sound escapes her lips.

I reach out, as careful as I can. My fingers brush her temple.

"Rosie," I whisper. "I'm here."

Slow and uncertain, her lashes flutter open. Her brows knit together.

"Rosie." I say again, my voice nothing but gravel and ache.

Her heavy, heat-drenched eyes blink open. Glassy, unfocused, and shining with tears.

For a second, she just stares at me like I'm not real. Like she's still lost somewhere in the burn, hallucinating me into existence.

I move closer, just my hand. Just enough to tuck her unruly brown curls behind her ear.

The second my fingers brush her skin and she exhales like she's been saved from drowning.

"Theron…?" she breathes.

My name on her lips almost undoes me.

"I'm here," I say gently. "Right here, baby."

A tear slides down her cheek. She doesn't even flinch when it hits the pillow.

"I thought…" Her voice cracks. "I thought I made you stay away."

My heart splinters.

"You didn't," I whisper. "Nothing could."

I shift at the edge of the bed, moving closer, still outside the perimeter of her nest. The boundary her body built when it was begging for safety, protection and *me*.

I don't dare invade that space, not yet.

It's hers.

And that is important.

I don't care if it's made of blankets filled with holes or wrinkled flat pillows or shirts I've worn threadbare. I won't cross it unless she invites me in.

So, I hold my breath, plant my hand on the mattress beside her, and ask.

"Rosie…may I come into your nest?"

She blinks.

The answer is instant. Even through her haze. She nods.

But then she whispers, broken and hoarse, "Please."

A shudder runs through me.

"Thank you," I say, because it matters.

Because it *should* matter.

No Alpha, no mate, should ever step into an Omega's nest without permission. Not when they're in heat. Not when they're vulnerable.

This space is sacred. Built by instinct, emotion, and love. A fortress made of scent and memory.

And she chose me to cross the threshold.

I move slowly, carefully, slipping into the ruined center of her world.

She whimpers the second my knees hit the nest. My scent floods the space like smoke and thunder, burning away the fever that tortured her for too long.

"I'm here," I whisper, reaching for her. "I've got you now."

She collapses into me as if gravity was winning the fight.

Her hands fist into my shirt and she presses her face to my chest with a sob that breaks my heart.

"It hurts," she whispers.

"I know," I breathe into her hair. "I know, baby. I'm going to take care of it. I'm going to take care of *you*."

She buries herself deeper, her limbs trembling like they've forgotten how to rest. And I hold her, tight yet gentle.

Wrapped around her like a promise.

She clings to me like I'm the only solid thing in the world. And maybe right now, I am.

Her breath comes in shudders. Small, broken things. But they begin to slow the moment my arms wrap tighter around her, anchoring her to me.

Her heat is overwhelming. Rolling off her in waves that sink teeth into my skin. My body responds instantly. Eager. Wild. But I leash the worst of it.

She doesn't need a beast.

Not yet.

I tilt her face toward me, cupping her cheek with one hand, thumb brushing along her damp skin. "Tell me what you need." I whisper.

Her eyes, red-rimmed and desperate, flutter up to meet mine.

"Please don't ever let me go through this alone again."

My heart shatters. It splinters, jagged and raw, right down the middle

I tuck her tighter into my chest, one hand sliding behind her head, the other trembling where it grips her waist.

"I won't," I whisper, throat thick. "Never again, baby. I promise."

She nods against me, silent tears wetting my collar.

And I can't take it. Not the guilt, not the scent of her pain wrapped in longing. Not the way her body trembles against mine like she doesn't believe I'm real yet.

So, I lean down, lips brushing the skin at her neck, right over the faint scar where I marked her all those years ago.

The bond mark.

The symbol of everything we are. Everything I promised her.

And I sink my teeth into it. Not hard enough to hurt, just enough to hold. Enough to remind her of our bond.

She gasps, her entire body arching into me as a moan trembles from her lips.

Her scent changes, just slightly. Less fear. More need.

She breathes out my name like a prayer. "Theron…"

"Yes, sweetheart?" I rasp, licking over the bite. I want her to tell me, to command me, to demand every filthy wish she could ever ask for.

Her fingers tighten in my shirt, tugging at the fabric until it stretches across my back. Her hips roll, barely a grind against my thigh. But I feel it.

"Alpha," she whimpers, hips rolling against me once more.

I growl, low and deep, then mouth my way down her throat, teeth scraping her skin without sinking in.

"You have to say it, Rosie." I murmur. "What do you want my Omega? What do you need?"

"You," she breathes, arching into me. "Please. Theron, please."

I kiss her. *Finally.*

Our mouths crash like storm waves, all teeth and tongue and desperation. She tastes like salt and need, and pure fucking addiction.

My hands start to roam, sliding over soft curves and trembling skin, but I pause when I feel the tight stretch of fabric beneath my palms.

She's wearing one of my shirts.

It's too tight. Clinging to her like it doesn't quite belong, sleeves stretched around her upper arms and the hem is caught just below her hips. Omegas don't usually nest with clothes on, but she kept this one on.

My shirt.

"Why is this still on you?" I ask gently, pulling back just enough to brush the collar with my fingers. "You're supposed to be bare, baby."

Her cheeks flush deeper, shame flickering across her expression as her hands move to tug at the hem.

"I just… I needed something. Anything that felt like you." Her voice is a whisper, cracking at the edges. "I—I know it's dumb, but it was the closest I could get to feeling like your hands were on me."

Fuck.

My heart twists again.

I sink down, kissing the cotton fabric over her belly, letting my lips linger there as my hands slide under the hem. I lift it slowly, reverently, baring inches of warm skin beneath.

"Not dumb," I murmur, kissing higher. "Not even close."

She arches slightly, breath hitching as I peel the shirt over her head and toss it aside.

"There you are," I whisper, drinking in every inch of her. Her soft belly. Her flushed chest. Every part of her trembling for me, slick and wanting and real.

"Perfect," I rasp, reverence in every syllable. "You're fucking perfect."

She reaches for me. My hand. My body. Anything.

And I give it all.

Because she's mine.

And it's time to remind her exactly what that means.

CHAPTER 8
THERON

She lies bare beneath me now. Soft curves glowing in the dim light, skin flushed and slick with heat, trembling under my gaze.

She's never looked more beautiful.

My girl.

My Omega.

Her body calls to me, every inch of her marked by desperate desire, and some lingering shadow of pain I'm going to erase. Slowly. Worshipfully. Thoroughly.

I let my eyes trail from the slope of her shoulders down to her plush thighs, my hands following the same path in slow, tender strokes. Her breasts rise and fall with each trembling breath, and I press kisses there, whispering praise against her skin between each one.

"So beautiful," I mumble, lips skimming her skin. "Every soft, sweet part of you was made for me."

She gasps when I mouth gently at her hip, arching under the touch. My hands splay across her waist, sinking into her flesh like I can hold every part of her at once. She doesn't shy away from it, not anymore. She lets me touch her like this, lets me love her body with all the hunger yet with the tenderness I've been carrying since the first time I saw her.

And I want her to see me, too.

I sit back onto my heels, fingers moving to the buttons of my shirt, the ache in my cock nearly unbearable as I strip away the layers between us.

But as I start to toss the shirt aside, she reaches for it.

"Wait," she says, voice barely more than a breath.

Her fingers close around the fabric. She holds it to her chest for a moment, then reaches toward the edge of the nest and tucks it there, nestled between a pillow and one of her many blankets. It's deliberate. Instinctual. Sacred.

Then she reaches for my jacket. My belt. My pants.

One by one, she removed each piece from my body, adding them into the nest like offerings. Like anchors.

My chest tightens at the sight. At the devotion.

She's rebuilding it around us. Around my scent.

My pride burns bright in my chest, mingling with the sharp edge of arousal and fierce unadulterated love.

She bends forward to place my jeans against the edge of her makeshift wall, and my gaze drops immediately.

Her ass, full and flushed, is on full display, slick dripping between her thighs, and my cock twitches at the sight before me.

I reach out, letting my fingers trace the curve of her ass with gentle appreciation. Her breath catches, but she doesn't stop me. If anything, she arches slightly, presenting herself like it's the most natural thing in the world.

"Beautiful," I rasp, letting my hand slide lower, dragging my fingers through the wet heat between her folds. She gasps and her knees tremble as she braces herself on the edge of the nest.

"Alpha!"

"I've got you," I murmur, pressing a soft kiss to the small of her back. "Just like this. Let me take care of you."

I slip two fingers inside her. Her pussy is soaking, hot, and tight. The moan she gives me is worth every hour, every mile, every moment I spent away from her.

She keeps working, arms moving with instinct as she tucks the last of my clothes into her nest, all while my fingers curl inside her, stroking slow and steady, coaxing more slick from her trembling body.

It's the strangest, most perfect moment.

A quiet blend of connection, devotion, and raw, slow-burning lust.

She shudders around my fingers, soft moans echoing off the walls. I plunge them deeper, pressing into the tender spot I know drives her wild.

"Alpha," she gasps, the word breaking in half, torn between pleasure and panic.

I nuzzle the curve of her ass, kissing her spine. "Let go for me. You need this. You've needed it so bad, haven't you?"

She nods frantically, her hips rolling to meet each slow thrust of my hand, and I growl low in my chest at the sight of her. Her body starts to tighten, the trembling building toward something electric.

"That's it," I murmur, curling my fingers again. "Come for me, baby. Let it out."

Her cry is ragged and utterly beautiful.

She falls apart on my hand with a sob, her inner walls fluttering and clenching, dragging a broken moan from deep in her throat.

I don't stop. I don't dare. I work her through every last ripple of that release, coaxing more slick from her like honey from the comb.

But it's not enough.

I slide my fingers free, watching the way her slick clings to my hand like spun sugar. I bring them to my lips without hesitation. Like a hungry bear, I savor the taste of her honey. Salt and musk, and nothing like honey at all, but God, I can't get enough.

The flavor coats my tongue, and my cock throbs at the taste, at the way her body gave it to me so freely and still I want more.

Gently, I shift her.

"Easy, Rosie," I murmur, guiding her down onto her back. Her body is pliant, arousal dripping down her thighs as she lets me move her. I kiss her belly as I go, dragging my fingers down her sides, grounding her, holding her.

I settle between her legs, spreading her thighs open with possessive hands. She gasps at the exposure, chest rising in shuddering breaths.

"Theron…" her voice breaks, raw and aching. "Please, it hurts."

"I know," I brush a kiss to the inside of her thigh. "I'm going to make it better."

I press my mouth to her weeping cunt and lick a long, slow stripe from her entrance to her clit, groaning as her taste hits my tongue, earthy and raw and so unmistakably hers. She jerks beneath me, sobbing into the open room as I lap at her, licking her like she's my personal honey pot.

My tongue circles her clit, then flicks fast, teasing and coaxing more of those symphonic cries. Her hips writhe, legs trembling on either side of my head. I grip her thighs tighter, spreading her open, keeping her there. Right where I want her. Right where she needs to be.

My hand slips between us again and I press those same two fingers back inside her pussy. She lets out a strangled sob, her back arching off the bed.

"Alpha!" she cries, voice fractured.

"Come for me," I growl against her delicious cunt, the vibration making her cry out again.

My fingers drive deeper, her moans growing louder. My mouth stays locked on her clit, flicking and sucking, my fingers working in and out of her tight, swollen cunt, my tongue stroking that bundle of nerves causing her body to shake uncontrollably.

A broken moan rips from her throat, wild and raw and wrecked.

"Theron! I'm—" she pants, her hands fisting the sheets.

"That's it," I rasp between licks. "Give it to me, Rosie. Let go."

She's shattering like glass in my hands.

She breaks apart so beautifully, thighs shaking around my head, her orgasm crashing through her with violent, unrestrained need. She sobs my name, her voice going hoarse, and I drink her down like I need it to survive.

Only when she starts to twitch, overstimulated and sensitive, do I finally pull back.

Her body quivers.

Used, swollen, flushed from unrelenting bliss.

But not satisfied.

And neither am I.

I crawl up the length of her, kissing a trail from her soaked core to her belly, up to her heaving chest. Her arms reach for me, weak but wanting, and I brace my weight carefully above her, settling between her thighs.

Our eyes lock.

Her pupils are blown wide, lips red from biting them, her face red with effort and heat. But there's clarity there too. A clear need.

"Please," she whimpers. "Please, Alpha."

I rock forward with a growl, cock breaching her swollen pussy in one brutal thrust answering her pretty pleas.

She screams, high and wrecked, and it's the sweetest fucking sound I've ever heard. I drive in until I'm buried to the hilt, my hips grinding against hers, my cock locked in heat-swollen velvet.

Fuck.

She's perfect.

Tight. Hot. Clenching like her body's been waiting for this. *For me.*

"Mine," I snarl, voice half-feral, and sink my teeth into her throat.

Not the bond mark. Not yet.

She wails beneath me, hips rocking back, begging for more with every tremble of her body. Her scent shifts, no longer fear or sadness, but pure *lust and worship*. A siren's call meant only for me.

My hands clamp down on her hips, fingers digging in so hard I know there'll be bruises. I want there to be bruises. I *want* her marked by me, both inside and out. Proof she's mine and only mine.

I pull out just enough to feel her whimper, then slam back in, hard and deep, the way she needs.

The way we both *need.*

Her moans are raw, loud, unfiltered cries that echo off the bedroom walls, a perfect chorus of need and surrender.

"More Alpha, more! Don't stop. Don't you dare *fucking* stop."

My face twists with a greedy, hungry grin and I'm sure I look like an absolute fool, but I'm her fool.

My rhythm is brutal. Primal. The sound of skin slapping, and her breathless screams fills the whole house. My cock drags against every sensitive nerve of her pussy, driving her higher and higher. Her nails rake down my arms, her back arches, and she sobs like she's dying of pleasure.

"You *feel* that?" I growl into her ear, one hand fisting in her hair, the other dragging her hips harder into mine. "That's what you were begging for."

"Yes, yes, *Theron!*"

Her words cut off in a scream as I slam into her again, and her body clamps down, pulsing tight around me.

She's close.

So close.

I growl again, feral and rough, as I bite into her shoulder and fuck her through it. No mercy, no pause, just thrust after thrust until her body seizes. She clenches around me, every muscle going tight like a drawn bowstring.

She *breaks.*

Her wail rips through the room, her orgasm crashing into her like a fucking tidal wave. She shatters on my cock, shouting my name like it's the only word she knows. The walls of her pussy milking me so hard I see stars.

I growl, teeth dragging over her throat as I drive into her, relentless, grinding her through the peak until she's sobbing and soaking the sheets, her slick spilling down my thighs.

She's perfect like this, wild, wrecked, and ruined.

But I'm far from done.

I pull out.

"No!" Her voice breaks, frantic and raw. "Don't, please don't. Alpha, don't stop!"

"*Rosie.*"

My voice cuts through her panic, ruthless and commanding.

She stills.

Breathing ragged. Body shaking. But still.

"Turn around," I say, slower now, deep and rough. "On your knees. Hands down, ass up. I want to see you. Present for me, baby."

She shakes her head, moaning, still chasing the last tremor of her release.

I cup her cheek, tilting her gaze up to mine.

"Be a good girl and you'll get every inch. Every drop." I kiss her cheek chasing away those tray tears. "I'm going to breed you just the way your body's begging me to."

She shudders, lips parting in a whimper.

"Do as I say, Omega."

She nods. "Y-Yes."

"Good girl."

It takes her a moment. Her limbs unsteady, her breath catching, but she does as I ask.

She rolls onto her front, lifts onto her knees, and presses her chest to the nest, face turned to the side, her blushing cheek against a sweat-soaked pillow. Her ass rises, hips tilted back.

God damn.

It's the most beautiful thing I've ever seen.

My Omega.

Laid bare, offered up and *ready.*

I palm myself, lining up behind her, the head of my cock already thick and swollen with the promise of the knot that's coming.

Her scent floods me, ripe, eager, pleading.

"My good little Omega," I murmur, guiding myself to her arousal coated pussy.

CHAPTER 9
ROSIE

Theron thrusts back inside me in one brutal, perfect stroke.

I scream.

Not from pain.

From *relief*.

From the hot, staggering stretch of his cock splitting me open, forcing my body to take every inch, every vein, every brutal promise of what he's about to do to me.

"Oh my God!"

My voice shatters as he bottoms out, his hips grinding flush to my ass, the thick head of his cock seated deep, so deep it aches in the best possible way. He's so *big*. My body flutters around him, struggling to adjust, slick gushing from me like I've waited a *lifetime* for this moment.

My fingers claw at the bedding, fists curled into the blankets of the nest I built for *him*. For us.

"*Alpha…*" I gasp, my arms trembling beneath me, face buried in the blankets of our nest.

"*Fuck*, baby," Theron groans behind me, voice wrecked and reverent. "So tight. So wet. This perfect little cunt, she missed me, didn't she?"

He rolls his hips. Just once. Slow and deep, dragging every thick inch against my swollen walls. My body seizes, toes curling, heat licking across my skin like fire. I gasp, half-sobbing, overwhelmed already.

I whimper, nodding, hips rocking back against him, greedy for more.

His hands slide up my sides, warm and grounding, fingers dragging along the soft curve of my waist before gripping my hips, firm, but not rough. Possessive. Anchoring.

"I've thought about this," he says, his voice lower now, rasping like it hurts to speak through the need. "About you like this. Bent over, dripping for me. *Carrying me.*"

My breath hitches.

"I've dreamed about it," he admits, thrusting deep again, and I feel the shudder that rolls through him. "Your belly round, full with our baby. Still begging for my knot. So fucking pretty, so *mine.*"

God, he's going to break me.

He pulls almost all the way out, only to push back in with a groan so deep it rumbles against my spine. I moan, the friction unbearable, every movement feeding the burn low in my belly.

"Greedy little thing," he murmurs. "So good for me. So fucking perfect." He bends lower, his chest brushing my back, lips ghosting the shell of my ear. "Tell me what you want, Omega. Tell me what this hungry cunt's aching for."

"You," I sob. "Your knot. Your come. I want to be full. I want to be bred, please. *Alpha*, please."

He groans like I just fed him something holy, like he's never heard anything sweeter than me begging to be *bred*.

And God help me, I mean every word.

He curses, hips snapping forward hard enough to steal the air from my lungs.

"That's it," he snarls, feral and breathless. There's no softness left, only hunger. Obsession. *Claim*.

He slams into me, harder, deeper—his cock dragging against every swollen, aching spot inside me, his knot thickening, catching, threatening to lock us together. I sob beneath him, unable to do anything but *feel*.

His grip on my hips tightens, fingers bruising into my flesh like he's trying to brand me. His teeth scrape down my shoulder, then clamp down at the base of my neck—right above the bond mark. Like a warning. A promise.

He's panting like a beast, hot and ragged and completely *gone*.

I can feel it—how close he is. The way his cock throbs, the way his knot bulges, desperate to catch. The low, relentless growl rumbling from his chest, vibrating against my back like thunder.

My body tightens, the orgasm building fast, out of control, fueled by the filthy sounds of him using me, the wet slap of our bodies, the possessive snarl with every thrust.

He drives forward, hips jerking as he buries himself *deep*, and everything inside me *snaps*.

I shatter with a scream, pleasure ripping through me so violently I can't even breathe.

With a final, devastating thrust, he locks inside me.

His knot swells, catching hard, sealing us together.

I wail, high and wrecked, as the thick stretch forces my body wider, finally giving my heat the pressure it's craved, and needed. The ache eases just enough to make me cry harder. Relief and sensation mixing in a dizzying flood through my body.

But he doesn't come.

He snarls against the back of my neck and keeps moving with short, grinding thrusts that send jolts of pressure blooming through my overstimulated body. Every shift of his hips rocks the knot against the edge of pain and pleasure, teasing deeper, rougher, wilder.

His cock throbs, trapped inside me. Needy. Furious.

"You feel that?" he pants, voice shredded with lust. "That stretch? That's me, baby. That's my knot keeping you open, exactly where I want you."

I sob, unable to answer, too full to do anything but shake beneath him.

He groans, biting down, just shy of breaking skin, his breath harsh in my ear.

"Not done yet," he grits out. "Not until I feel you melt around me. Not until I'm so deep inside you, you'll dream about it."

My walls clench, more slick flooding around the knot, and he ruts harder, chasing the high he's holding just out of reach. The tension coils tighter in his frame, in his voice, in the way he can't stop moving.

He's unhinged.

Lost.

Feral.

And so fucking close.

I feel it when it hits him. That split-second falter. The ragged growl. The full-body tremble.

His hips jerk once. Twice.

Then he growls, low, guttural, almost pained, as his cock kicks inside me.

The first pulse of release is hot. Devastating. The next is deeper. Stronger. Like it's claiming something buried inside me.

He buries himself deep, snarling through clenched teeth as he unloads. Thick, molten ropes of come flooding my womb, pumping past the swell of his knot with brutal force. My cunt clenches again, milking every drop, my body weeping slick around the tie, overwhelmed and sated.

He pants against my skin, breath hot and shaking. I feel him tremble, like even he can't believe I'm still here, still his, still taking every drop.

His voice is ruined when he says it:

"Mine."

It's not a question. Not a plea.

Just fact.

A sacred, snarled truth.

And then his teeth sink into the bond mark.

Not gently.

Not carefully.

He *claims* it.

A full rebrand, jaw clenched, bite deep, sealing what was already his with a renewed, vicious vow that makes my whole-body jolt.

The sensation detonates inside me like a bomb.

I scream, voice raw as another orgasm crashes through me. More intense than the last. My cunt tightens around his knot, pulsing, sucking, *clinging* to him like I never want to let go. Like I *can't*.

I feel his groan more than hear it. Low and feral, rumbling against my back as he bites harder, holding me there, holding *us* there, caught between agony and ecstasy.

He's still coming.

Still locked.

Still so deep inside me I can't tell where I end and he begins.

And when he finally releases the bite, laving over the mark with a possessive tongue, I'm gone.

Spent.

Shaking.

Breathing his name like a benediction.

His arms wrap around me, pulling me down into the nest, his knot still caught, still anchoring us together.

I'm wrecked.

Filled. Claimed. Owned.

So is he.

And it's perfect.

Because I'm completely, irrevocably his.

CHAPTER 10
ROSIE

I don't know how long we lay there, tied, trembling, breath tangled like the rest of our bodies. The ache has dulled to something slow and warm, a simmering weight deep in my belly. His knot is still locked inside me, pulsing gently every so often, like his body isn't ready to stop claiming me.

And honestly I don't want it to.

His arms are wrapped around me, chest flush to my back, every inch of him pressed against me like he's afraid I'll vanish. I can feel his lips moving against my shoulder—sweet, loving kisses, one after the other. Between them, I think I hear him whisper.

Mine. Mine. Mine.

My eyes are heavy, but my heart won't settle. Not yet. Not when every pulse of his knot makes me ache all over again.

"Theron." I breathe, voice ruined, barely more than a hum in the nest.

He grunts softly behind me. "I'm here, baby."

His hand strokes down my arm, trailing light touches from shoulder to wrist, like he's still grounding himself. Or maybe me.

"Did I hurt you?" he asks, quieter now.

"No," I whisper. "You put me back together."

A pause. His exhale is shaky, like he doesn't quite believe me.

I twist a little in his hold, feeling the way our bodies are still joined. We both groan, mine soft and tender, his low and gravelly.

"That wasn't supposed to happen like that," he mutters, kissing the curve of my neck. "I wanted to go slow. Be gentle."

"You were perfect," I tell him, reaching back to touch his face. "I needed all of it. Every growl. Every bite."

He nuzzles into my palm like he's starved for the softness. "I like the beard, by the way. It makes you look rugged." I tease and he laughs, and spouts some nonsense worried I wouldn't like it.

Eventually, his knot begins to soften. It takes time. We shift gently, limbs tangled, both of us whimpering as he finally slips free with a slow, wet stretch and a shared hiss of breath.

I feel the flood before I see it, his come and my slick dripping down my thighs, thick and warm. My body clenches like it wants to keep every drop.

"Fuck," he murmurs, catching it with his hand. "You're a mess."

I giggle, dazed and drunk on him. "Your fault."

He laughs, quiet, breathless, still shaken by it all.

"Come here," he says, lifting me gently. "Let me take care of you."

His arms slide under me, strong and sure, and I melt against him with a tired whimper. My legs dangle uselessly, too sore, too jelly-soft to carry me anywhere on my own. But Theron doesn't hesitate and carries me through the room like I weigh nothing, like I'm precious cargo he refuses to let go of.

The lights in the bathroom are soft, blending with the peaceful atmosphere from the bedroom. He nudges the door open with his hip and sets me carefully on the toilet seat.

"Just sit for me, sweetheart," he murmurs, brushing my damp tangled hair away from my face. "I'll make it nice."

He leans forward to start the shower, twisting the knobs until steam begins to rise and fills the space. The heat fogs the mirror, curling up into the corners of the room like a warm promise. I watch him through bleary eyes, his strong back, the muscles flexing beneath his skin, the way his hair is still mussed from our nest.

The smell of us is everywhere. Slick, sweat, heat, and sex. It clings to my skin and his. It's thick in the air, only made heavier by the steam.

When he turns back, his gaze softens instantly.

"You're still shaking," he says, dropping to one knee in front of me. "Let's get you cleaned up."

He helps me stand, steadying me with both hands around my waist. My knees buckle slightly, but he catches me, pulling me flush to his chest with a soft, proud rumble.

"I've got you," he whispers again. "Always."

He guides me slowly into the shower, one step at a time, until the water hits my skin. I gasp, part from the heat, part from the sting of sensitivity between my legs. But his hands are on me immediately, soothing, anchoring.

"Too hot?" he murmurs against my temple.

I shake my head. "No. It's perfect."

He hums low in his chest and presses a kiss to my damp hair. His hands begin to roam, not to claim this time, not to tease. Just to care. Gentle strokes over my arms, my back. He takes his time, washing me with such tenderness it makes my eyes sting.

Every pass of his hands is a reminder: *you're mine, and I love you enough to worship every inch of you.*

When he kneels again, washing between my thighs with infinite care, I whimper, nearly overwhelmed.

"You're so sore," he says, voice thick with guilt. "I went too hard."

I reach down, threading my fingers into his hair. "You didn't. I needed it. I wanted it."

His eyes flick up to mine, dark and reverent. "Still. Let me fix what I can."

I nod, and he kisses the inside of my thigh before standing once more, pulling me into his arms under the spray of water.

He cradles me there for what feels like forever, letting the hot water soak into our bones.

And for the first time since my heat began, I feel safe. Clean. Whole.

But the ache… The ache never really leaves.

Not when he's holding me like this.

Not when his cock is already starting to harden again, thick and pressing between us beneath the water.

Not when my heat, softened but not spent, begins to rise once more.

The hot water sluices down my back, easing some of the soreness. My muscles sigh with relief. But the ache between my legs is still there, deep and sweet and pulsing. Especially with him this close. Especially when I feel him stirring against me.

His cock is thickening, growing heavy and impossible to ignore. It presses against my ass, hot and insistent, even as his arms hold me close like I might break.

I shift a little in his embrace, just enough to press my hips back against him, grinding in a slow, gentle circle.

Theron freezes.

The rumble in his chest comes low and commanding. "Rosie."

I hum, tilting my head toward him. "Yes, Alpha?"

I feel him groan more than hear it. His grip on my hips tightens, just for a second, and I know he's close to snapping. The beast inside him is pacing again, waking back up now that I'm rubbing against him like I want to be filled all over again.

Because I do.

But instead of grabbing me, pinning me to the wall and sinking back inside my begging cunt, he pulls away slightly. Enough to put space between us.

"Baby," he says, voice strained and still full of that low heat, "you need a moment."

I blink, the heat haze not yet fully cleared from my brain. "But I—"

"You're still shaky," he murmurs, brushing his knuckles along my thigh. "And that bed…" He lets out a breath through his nose, eyes narrowing slightly. "Those sheets are destroyed. And your poor nest is barely hanging on."

That stops me.

My body jolts with something instinctive.

He watches the shift happen in real time, how I go from playful to hyper-focused. How my hands tighten at my sides.

"The nest…" I murmur, nearly breathless. "It's ruined."

"It needs to be rebuilt," he says gently, nuzzling against my jaw. "We'll build it together. With fresh blankets and my scent. And yours."

My pulse jumps, that primal pull stirring inside me again.

I want him. God, I *want* him. But I *need* that space. That place where I can pull him close and wrap around him like I'll never let go.

"I need it," I whisper. "I need my nest, Theron."

"I know," he says, already reaching for a towel. "We'll fix it, baby. I'll help. But first, we dry off. And you let me carry you back."

His hands are already moving with purpose. Gently blotting my skin, wrapping me up in the towel, and kissing my shoulder with aching care.

And I let him. Because he's right.

The nest comes first.

But the moment it's remade, he's mine again.

And this time, I won't let him leave until I've taken everything I desire.

CHAPTER 11
ROSIE

It's been a little over three weeks since my heat broke.

Three weeks of recovery. Of quiet mornings and slow walks. Of Theron wrapping me in his arms like I might vanish if he let go.

In fact, he's become almost too attached.

Just last night, he buried his face in my neck and hummed something under his breath. "You smell sweeter lately."

His words were whispers, like little sweet nothings spoken between kisses and cuddles. "Like warm muffins, or fresh bread pulled right out of the oven. It's driving me crazy."

He kissed me, and held me, breathing me in like I was a comfort he would never want to let go of.

And maybe it was just sweet words. Maybe I'm overthinking it. But I've been so tired lately.

My body feels bloated and sore, like a balloon ready to pop and fatigue, that I can't nap away.

And then there's the spiral of thoughts. They stir something dangerous in my chest. Something fragile and foolish.

Could I be? Is it possible? What if?

And hope is a slippery, painful thing. And I don't let myself fall for it easily.

Because I've been here before.

Looking into every symptom, like a golden sign. Tired. Achy. Breast tenderness. The usual signs that get your heart skipping when you want something badly enough.

And every time, it's a no.

A crumpled test in the trash.

An ache in my heart.

A tear I pretend not to wipe away before Theron walks in.

I know what this is. I know the rhythm of disappointment.

So when I pull the test from the cabinet and pee into a plastic cup, why do I still hope?

Why do I torture myself with another test?

Why does my heartbeat with excitement even though I don't believe?

Why do I pray to a silent God that I won't have to temper Theron's hope before it can take root again.

He never says it out loud. But I see it.

Every time he brushed his fingers over my stomach.

Every time his hand lingers there too long in the middle of the night.

Every time he watches another mated pair walk by with a stroller and gets quiet.

I hate how much I still hope.

Even after I've tried to bury it.

The test sits on the counter. Face-down. Waiting.

I haven't flipped it yet.

I hear footsteps behind me. The slow, heavy gait of the only man whose presence makes me feel lighter.

"Baby?" Theron's voice is quiet, curious. "You okay?"

I don't answer and lean against the sink, arms crossed, staring down at nothing.

With a now clean-shaven face, he stands in the doorway, and perceptively notices the test before I can say anything, or try to hide it, not that I really even try to.

He joins me in the bathroom, arms trapping me on both sides as he braces the sink I rest on.

He presses a kiss to my shoulder. "You don't have to check. We don't have to do this right now."

I shake my head. "I want to get it over with."

I feel the hope in him like a heartbeat. Quiet. Constant.

When I don't move, he nudges gently, guiding me until I look at him. He pulls me into his lap as he sits on the closed toilet lid, his arms locked tight around my waist.

"It's okay," he murmurs. "If it's not this time…it will be soon."

I close my eyes.

"Don't say that."

"Why?" His voice is warm against my skin. "Because I believe it?"

"Because I don't want to feel it." I press my forehead to his. "I don't want to hope and then feel that drop in my stomach again. I don't want to see it on your face when it's another no."

He tilts my chin up gently. Kisses me once. Soft. Full of that relentless tenderness that both soothes and hurts.

"It's not a no," he says quietly. "It's just not today."

I bite my lip, trying to hold the words down, but they slip out anyway.

"I want it so bad, Theron."

"I know."

His hands stroke along my sides, soothing me. "Me too."

And then, because he always finds a way to break me in the softest way, he says, "I dream about it, you know. Your belly round with stretch marks you'll call ugly, while I call them beautiful."

I nudge him, at the mention of stretch marks, like I don't have enough of those.

"You'll be glowing and grumpy and nesting like a queen while I spoil you rotten."

A shaky laugh breaks out of me.

"Glowing and grumpy?"

"Oh yeah. Mean as hell. You'll send me out for cookies and cry when I bring the wrong ones. Only to send me back out for some other craving you have."

I smile, because yeah, I could see that happening too. I press a kiss to the corner of his mouth.

His smile is warm, like a ray of sunshine breaking through the clouds after a downpour of rain, and it helps. God, it always helps.

But the test is still waiting.

And I can't take this not knowing.

I untangle from his lap and move to the counter.

I flip the test over.

And the world falls quiet.

Two lines.

Two.

My vision tunnels. My chest squeezes like something's locked around it.

I think I might pass out.

My knees almost give out, but the only thing that falls, are tears.

"Rosie?" His voice is sharp with worry. "It's okay. We can always try next time."

I laugh, tears still falling and then I show him the test. I just hold it up in a shaking hand.

His eyes scan it. Once. Twice.

And then he goes still.

"Is that…?"

I nod.

Tears fall like a damn waterfall down my cheeks.

"It's positive."

He doesn't breathe for a second. Just stares at it like it might vanish if he blinks. And I can't blame him. I can't look away either.

He laughs.

A choked, stunned, wild laugh that bursts out of his chest as he pulls me in.

"Baby," he says, voice shaking, arms tight around me. "Oh God, baby. We did it."

I cling to him. Crying. Laughing. Drenched in disbelief.

He's still staring at the second pink line. A bewildered crazy smile on his face that suddenly morphs into a serious one.

"We need a new house."

I blink. "What?"

He turns to me, eyes wide, glowing, a little wild. "A new house. With a yard and, and more rooms."

"Theron," I breathe, still too stunned to feel the floor under my feet. "We can just change the library back into a nursery—"

"No." The word is firm, full of conviction. He steps closer, cupping my face in both hands. "No, baby. You deserve more than that. You deserve a real space. Not a compromise. We've outgrown this house and it's time for something new."

His words shake me. Something new sounds great and yet I'm filled with doubt, because it feels like that amazing little pink line will just fade away. And that gut wrenching feeling of despair will swallow me whole again. And my grip on joy is slipping away, second by second.

Theron's smile is radiant, forehead brushing mine. "The next one will have room for us. For the baby. For the others who might come someday," his hopeful voice is sweet, filled with a hopeful dream of lots of little ones filling our home with noise and love.

God, I want to feel what he feels. But I don't know if I can just yet. There have been too many *nos*, too many negative tests that have turned my rose-tinted dreams into gray numbness.

"You'll have your dream kitchen. A bigger library. A tub big enough to fuck in." I slap his chest, his vulgar comment.

"A nursery filled with morning light. It's time for our dream home, Rosie."

My throat tightens. My hand curls over my belly like I'm trying to hold something in place, forbidding it from slipping away.

For half a second, I let myself imagine it. A tiny heartbeat. A warm weight in my arms. Theron pressed to my belly, whispering to someone only we can feel.

And then the fear swallows it whole.

The test is still on the bathroom counter. Two lines. Clear as day.

But my chest aches like I'm already mourning them.

Because what if it's not real?

What if it doesn't stick?

What if something goes wrong inside me? With the baby? With everything?

What if this hope is just a cruel joke, and I let myself believe too soon?

Theron's still talking, voice giddy, painting a future in broad, golden strokes. And I want to stand in it with him.

I do.

But all I can see is how far away that sunlit dream feels.

I nod when he kisses me. I smile when he pulls me close. But inside, storm clouds gather, shadowing this ray of light.

Because joy like this always feels like a countdown.

And I don't know how to stop the clock.

CHAPTER 12
THERON

Pregnant.

My mate is pregnant.

After years of trying, of shut doors and broken hearts.

Finally.

Pride fills my chest, but it's like nothing I've ever felt before. Nothing compares to this bone-deep, instinct-gnawing pride of knowing my Omega is carrying our child.

I bred my mate. Filled her until her body took root with mine.

My seed, planted deep, blooming inside the woman I'd burn the world for.

Our baby.

We did that.

As a mated pair we created this gift.

As a pair we marked each other. Claimed each other.

I made her mine in the most intimate of ways and she made me hers.

And God help me, I've never felt more whole.

"My perfect, sweet mate. Everything is about to change. Every wish we made. Every prayer we said. Every little curl and laugh we saw in our dreams. It's finally happening." My voice is low, giddy with each word. Each syllable.

But in my mate's eyes is a shadow. A cloud. It hovers over her and darkens the color of her brown eyes.

Fear.

And I know why. I know exactly why that fear sits in her eyes like a vile demon.

After every heat she held her breath, hoping that moment would be *the* time. Every test she took alone in the bathroom with shaking hands and a heart full of fragile hope.

And every time she stepped out with a quiet, broken look and a single pink or blue line staring up at her.

I remember the doctor's appointment. The way she smiled politely when they talked about odds and timing and "trying not to stress."

How she came home and cried in the shower, thinking I couldn't hear.

I heard every sob. Felt every hollow ache in her body like it was carved into mine.

So yes, I know where that fear comes from.

But this is no time for fear. This fleeting moment is something to celebrate, to share in this joy, and I plan to do just that.

I plan to chase those fears away, with my lips, my tongue, and these unrelenting hands that know her body better than I know my own. I'll kiss the doubt right off her skin, touch her until she forgets how to be afraid. I'll cover her in worship until she sees herself the way I do.

Until the clouds in her eyes scatter and all that's left is the light I know is still in there.

"Let me worship you, Rosie. Let me praise you." I kiss her, hunger stirring in my proud heart.

She gives me the slightest nod as I kiss her. And it's enough of a yes that I lift her into my arms and carry her to our bed.

She doesn't argue. Doesn't flinch. Just melts into me like she's being put back together.

I lay her down in the center of the bed and crawl over her like a starving man.

"You know what this means, don't you?" I ask, kissing the line of her throat.

She breathes out, shuddering. "What?"

"You're mine."

She laughs, "I've been yours for six years."

"No, not like this," I lick over her bond mark, the scarred bite a beautiful reminder of the past.

"This is so much more."

My teeth scrape against her throat, my hands stroke her sides, greedy for skin. I push her shirt up and she lets me take it, arms rising over her head. Her chest is bare, soft and blushing a pretty shade of red.

"Look at you," I murmur, palming her breasts. "God, you are beautiful, but just think how much more beautiful you'll be in a few weeks."

Her breath stutters as I gently pull at her hardened peaks. The color of her areola is still a dusty pink but soon they'll darken, and her breast will swell.

My mouth waters at just the thought.

She makes a sound like she wants to protest, but I refuse to let her.

I feel like I'm in battle against an invisible foe. A shadow in her mind, the doubt twisting this moment into something fragile. The fear that history will repeat itself.

It's throwing punches with her resistance, and no matter how tightly I hold her, I can't wrestle that what-if from her thoughts.

I lower my head and take one aching nipple into my mouth, tongue rolling gently, coaxing a whimper from her lips.

"You are going to be such a good mama," I murmur against her skin. "I can already see it. You'll glow, sweetheart."

A tiny gasp escapes her. With a slight tremble, her hands find my hair.

"I'll spoil you," I promise. "You'll wake up with my baby kicking inside you and me curled around your back." My mouth moves to her other nipple, leaving a trail of kisses across her chest.

"Everyday I'll talk to your belly. I'll tell our baby how much I love them and how good of a mama they have."

My tongue laves over her taut nipple and I'm not sure if the shaky breath that leaves her is from my words or my tongue.

"You'll waddle and curse and snap at me, and I'll just kiss you through the abuse."

She laughs. Breathless. Almost bashful. But it's there again, a quick flicker of guilt behind her eyes.

I don't give it the attention I'm sure it deserves and instead kiss my way down her belly.

"I'll never stop touching you," I murmur. "Not now. Not ever. You're the one thing I crave most in this world, Rosie."

Her thighs fall open for me like they always do, trusting, ready, *mine*. Before settling between them I drag her skirt and panties away. The soft, needy whine she makes as I pull her panties down makes my cock twitch in response.

"Shh, don't worry baby. I'm going to fuck you, just after I eat your pussy." I lick a long, slow stripe up her slit, groaning at the taste.

She moans hands flying to her mouth like she's ashamed of the sounds, but I growl low, dragging her hand away.

"Don't you dare. No hiding, not from me, mate." I drag my tongue against her again, adding pressure against her clit and watch in satisfaction as she moans once again.

"I'm going to eat you like you're the only thing keeping me alive," I growl again, this time louder, "and then I'm going to fuck you so full of praise, you'll never forget just how much I fucking love you."

She's already dripping for me, pussy slick and fluttering around nothing.

I devour her. Slow at first. Just savoring the intoxicating taste of my Omega.

The taste is different. Subtle. Addicting in a way that's nearly dangerous. She was already my addiction, but this? This is like switching from cocaine to heroin.

My tongue is relentless, lapping at her folds and swirling around her clit. My fingers teasing her until she's begging, panting, and finally shattering against my mouth.

I crawl back over her, cock hard, straining against my jeans, and my sweet girl is already reaching for my zipper, and pulling me out.

"You're mine." I push into her with a groan, sinking deep.

She arches, whimpers, clutches at me. "Alpha."

I pump into her—long, thick strokes that make her eyes flutter but she's already so wrecked, so wet and twitching, it only takes a few thrusts before she's breaking again, sobbing my name like a prayer.

God, my mate was made for this.

But I need more. I crave more. To knot her.

I whisper with each hard thrust.

"You're everything." *Thrust.*

"You're perfect." *Thrust.*

"You're going to give me a baby." *Thrust.*

Again, her orgasm rips through her like a wave. A scream of ecstasy fills the room as she clings to me, body pulsing around me in broken bliss.

I don't last much longer, my knot swelling thick and catching inside her tight cunt. I spill inside her with a roar, hips jerking, arms caging her in like I can brand her with the force of my love.

And as I hold her, still buried inside her warmth, still tasting the edges of her breath, I feel it again. That hum. That bone-deep knowing.

She's mine.

And she's carrying my future.

CHAPTER 13
ROSIE

The fluorescent light above me buzzes in uneven spurts, the rhythm off just enough to be irritating. Or maybe it's me. Everything feels like too much lately. Every sound, every thought, every beat of my heart that dares to whisper *what if?*

My thighs stick to the vinyl seat. The air is too cold, but my palms won't stop sweating. Every time someone coughs across the room, I jump.

I've always hated going to the doctor. It makes me feel small. Powerless. Like a kid being dragged somewhere they don't understand.

I've known Dr. Bryant for nearly a decade now. She's kind. Direct. Plus-sized like me, with deep brown skin that glows like polished mahogany, thick black curls framing her face and warm brown eyes that somehow always know when you're lying to yourself. She's never once made me feel small or broken or overly emotional. Not when I asked about fertility. Not when I sobbed through exams. Not even the time I broke down after a false positive.

She's good. Safe.

And I still feel like I'm about to vomit.

I called as soon as Theron loosened his hold on me, even as sweet and suffocatingly joyful as it was. My hands were shaking so bad I had to dial twice. The receptionist chirped out her congratulations before I could stop her, and I wanted to scream.

Because I don't know if it's real yet. Because I don't want it jinxed. Because I'm scared this is all a dream, and I'm going to wake up bleeding.

Theron was practically vibrating when I told him about the appointment. He even tried to come with me, not that I should be surprised, but I told him I wanted to do this part alone. I needed space to think. To breathe. To process.

He looked hurt. Not angry. Just a bit confused.

Like he couldn't fathom why I wouldn't want him there, grinning like he's already picked out names, which, of course he has.

I envy that—his wonderful ability to just believe.

For me, every moment since that pink line appeared has felt like walking a tightrope. One shaky breath away from falling.

A nurse calls a name, not mine, but I glance up anyway, hands clutching the clipboard in my lap like it might anchor me to the vinyl chair.

The walls here are beige. Cold. Nothing like the warmth of my library where I would nest, but even that felt wrong last month.

I press a hand to my stomach.

Soft and round like always but still silent.

Are you really in there?

I wish this could be like the movies or those clips on social media that always make me cry.

I want to feel it.

I want to know, deep in my heart, in my bones, in my soul that *you're real.* That every breath I take is for *you.* That every bite I take, every breath I draw, is being shared between *you and I.*

Please be real.

Please.

"Rose Blackwood?" I flinch at the sound of my name, stuck to my seat like a deer in headlights.

Again, the nurse calls my name and this time I stand, forcing my legs to move even though they feel like they've been dipped in cement.

The nurse is young, probably a Beta. Cheerful in a way that doesn't match the knot in my chest.

She offers me a smile I can't return and gestures for me to follow.

We stop at the scale. Of course.

"Just step up when you're ready," She chirps, tapping the metal bar like it's nothing. Like it hasn't ruined my day more than once.

I step up and the number climbs.

286.4

It used to devastate me. Used to feel like a branding. Like failure spelled in blinking red.

But that was before Theron.

Before the first time he dropped to his knees in front of me and kissed the softest part of my stomach like it was beautiful.

Before he called me gorgeous with his mouth buried between my thighs, and told me that Omegas like me—curvy, warm, soft—were built to be worshipped.

Still.

It's hard not to let the old ache bloom when that number stares back at me in a glaring shade of red.

"Okay, go ahead and have a seat in room three," the nurse says, scribbling something on her clipboard, most likely a concern about my obesity.

I trail behind her like a ghost.

Once inside, she goes through the motions, placing a blood pressure cuff on my arm and clipping an O2 sensor to my finger.

"What was the date of your last menstrual cycle?"

"I don't bleed regularly," I murmur. "I'm Omega."

"Oh! Sorry, right. Then, uh, last heat?"

"Eight weeks ago."

She makes a note.

"Have you had any spotting or cramps since?"

I shake my head.

"Any nausea? Tenderness? Mood changes?"

I nod once. All of the above.

Her pen scratches across the page like it's writing a fairytale I still don't believe in.

"Okay," she says, tucking her clipboard under her arm. "Dr. Bryant will be in shortly. You can undress from the waist down and cover with the drape if you're comfortable."

Then I'm alone.

The silence closes around me fast and I try not to look at the table. Or the paper sheet that'll crinkle under my weight. Or the corner where I cried three years ago after another failed heat.

Dr. Camellia Bryant had been gentle that day. Too gentle.

"I'm concerned, Rosie. You've had multiple unsuccessful heats in a row. I think it might be time to run some tests."

I'd nodded. Quiet. Willing. Until the tests came back.

Inconclusive.

Unremarkable.

Uncertain.

Like my body didn't even know what it was trying to do.

I remember her face. Warm. Apologetic. Offering me to use her nickname instead of the formal title of Doctor as she tried to find the right words to explain that sometimes even mated pairs, even healthy ones, just…don't align. That sometimes the rhythm is off. The bond too strong or not strong enough or… God, I don't even remember.

All I could hear was *broken*.

That was the day the guilt imbedded itself deep inside me. Shadowy tendrils sinking its hooks into every part of me.

That was the day I stopped being an Omega and started being a failure.

I was supposed to follow up. She gave me the number of a specialist. Slid it across the counter like an olive branch. Told me to take my time.

In the end, I never called. Never went.

Instead, I cried.

Cried until I was sick and sore and hoarse, screamed into a pillow until my throat felt shredded. Begged Theron not to make me do it. To not be analyzed and probed just to be told, I was broken. I was barely a woman, let alone an Omega.

And he didn't.

He held me, instead of forcing me to dial that damn number. Wrapped those big arms around me, pressed my face to his chest, and whispered how much he loved me. Not for what I could give him. Not for what my body failed to do. But because I was me.

Because I was his.

And for just a little while enveloped in his scent, tangled in the sheets and warm blankets, I forgot.

A soft knock on the door startles me and interrupts my brief solitude. The nurse pokes her head back in, holding a plastic cup with a label stickered across the side.

"Sorry, I almost forgot," she says brightly. "We'll need a urine sample today, too. Bathroom's right around the corner, take your time."

I take the cup with a nod and a quiet, "Thanks." A small part of me grateful for my spiraling thoughts. If I'd changed right away instead of wallowing in my self-pity, I might've been half-naked when she walked in.

As the door clicks shut again, I exhale slowly. Gathering the courage to rush down the hall and pee in the cup she handed me. Good thing I drank plenty of water this morning, I guess.

I manage the sample, wash up, and return to wait. Again.

This time with no interruption or dark spiraling of thoughts, I undress, folding my clothes and leaving them on the counter.

I shift awkwardly on the edge of the exam table, the crinkled paper sticking to the back of my thighs, tacky against my skin from nerves. My hands fidget with the sheet covering me from the waist below.

And I sit there. For what feels like forever. Waiting. And just as I'm about to get annoyed, another knock on the door comes and this time, it's her.

"Hey, stranger," Dr. Bryant greets as she steps inside, her voice warm as sunlight and twice as comforting. "Long time no see."

She hasn't changed a bit, still dressing in soft layers, her stethoscope draped around her neck like a necklace she forgot she was wearing. Her curls are pinned back today, a wide colorful headband holding them from her face. She smiles at me like I haven't aged a day.

"Hi, Millie," I murmur, and the sound of her nickname in my mouth almost makes me tear up.

She settles onto the stool beside me, flipping through the chart with her usual gentle efficiency

"Well," she says, tapping her pen once against the page. "The in-office test came back positive, too. Which means, your little one will be due November 12th." She says it so easily. With unshakable confidence. I can't move. Can't breathe.

It hits me slower than I expected, like warm honey pouring through my chest. A creeping warmth behind my ribs. My fingers clutch the sheet bunched around my waist. My breath stutters.

A broken laugh slips out of me. My hands fly to my belly, pressing gently over the round curve of skin that still shows nothing at all, except the size of my appetite.

My fingers splay over my belly, trembling. The paper crinkles beneath me, and for the first time all day, I let myself exhale all the way out. I want to sob. Or laugh. Or scream. But all I can manage is a whisper.

"You're real."

Oh God, you are real.

The threat of tears burns my eyes and the need to wrap myself in my Alpha with the confidence of Dr. Bryant's confirmation is almost overwhelming.

I almost regret not having Theron here. To relish in this with him.

But then again, it was probably a smart idea. That Alpha doesn't know the meaning of time and place.

Camellia pauses, just long enough to give that look. The one she gives patients who've fought too many quiet battles. The one that says *I know this has been hard* without saying anything at all.

But then she glances back down at the chart, her tone softening but turning clinical again.

"Rosie, I want to talk to you about a couple things." She sighs, possibly trying to gain the courage to most likely ruin my day.

"You're thirty now, and you're considered morbidly obese. That combination can sometimes increase your risk factors."

Yep. There it is.

My throat tightens, but I nod, acknowledging her concerns.

She's not being cruel. Just honest, as a doctor should be. But it still hurts like the truth always does. No matter how many times I've made peace with the way I'm built, it still lands like a slap when it's written in ink and whispered like a warning.

"I'm not worried," she adds quickly, meeting my eyes. "But I am cautious. I want to run a few tests today, just baseline bloodwork, hormone levels, that sort of thing. And I want you back here in about a month."

I nod again.

She reaches for a different sheet in the folder. "I've also gone ahead and scheduled your first ultrasound for two weeks from now. We'll want to confirm placement and viability."

I bite the inside of my cheek. *Viability*. The word sounds foreboding. Like a cliff edge. Like a test I haven't studied for.

It shouldn't feel heavy, like a weight on my shoulders, but it does.

Because that one word carries the weight of every question I still don't have answers to.

Is the heartbeat strong? Are you growing the way you should? Are you safe?

I don't know. There's still so much I don't know.

But this…this part is real.

You are real. And that truth steadies my quaking heart.

Dr. Bryant steps out for a moment and returns handing me a soft stack of folded papers with appointment times, nutrition recommendations and a list of supplements I should start right away. The prenatal pamphlet is glossy and full of smiling couples, hand -in-hand over pregnant bellies. It looks like a life I've wanted and now I'm closer than ever to it.

I run a finger over the edge of the ultrasound appointment, circled in blue pen.

Two weeks.

I'm giddy with the thought of seeing you. Maybe even hearing your little heartbeat. But I'll need to be patient.

"Go ahead and get dressed. A nurse will be here shortly to do your lab draws, and I will see you in a month." And with that, she was gone.

Just as Dr. Bryant said, a few minutes later, another nurse joins me after I finished dressing. She doesn't make small talk, just checks the orders, confirms my name, and asks me to roll up my sleeve.

The smell of antiseptic hits the back of my throat as she opens one of her many little swab packets and the cuff of my shirt tightens around my upper arm.

"I don't usually faint," I mutter, mostly to fill the awkward silence between us.

She hums, tying the blue band with care. "We'll be quick."

I nod. My gaze drifts to the corner of the room, where a framed poster lists hormone panels and thyroid checks and all the other things that might be swirling under the surface of my skin.

What if something's off?

What if I've gotten this far, just far enough to believe, and that hope gets torn away?

Don't.

I can't look for ghosts that aren't there. I can't constantly turn this dream into a nightmare, because then what is there to celebrate? What kind of mother will I be if all I ever do is flinch from the joy of it?

I try to breathe deep. Focus on the crinkle of paper under my thighs.

You're real, I remind myself again.

You're real. You're real.

But my heart still races—traitorous thing that it is,—and I wonder . *What would Theron say if he were here?*

He always knows what to say. Not in the polished, comforting way other people try to offer reassurance, but in the way that breaks through the panic and wraps around me like a weighted blanket.

He'd call me sweetheart.

He'd cup my cheek in those massive hands and look at me like there's not a single doubt in his mind.

He'd say I'm strong.

That my body won't fail.

That I was made to carry this life. Made to be loved. Made for him.

He'd growl it into my skin. Whisper it against my ear. He'd say it like a vow. *"You're mine, and nothing is going to take this from us."*

Just the thought of his voice, deep and sure, pulls the breath from my lungs like a prayer being answered.

I close my eyes and pretend his arms are already around me.

Just a little longer. Just hold on until I can get back to him. Until I can collapse in his arms and let him believe enough for the both of us.

The draw is over in a blink. A cotton ball. A bandage. A quiet thank you. The nurse exits just as silently as she came, and I'm left alone again.

Not entirely, though.

My hand settles over my belly, as if to shield the tiny, invisible thing inside me. As if my touch alone could keep it safe.

I stare at the door, a smile emerging from my face, and whisper into the quiet,

"Let's go home."

CHAPTER 14
THERON

"You're lucky I didn't fire your ass the moment I found out what you pulled."

Dominic Rourke's voice growls through the phone. I shift the phone to my other ear and glance out the kitchen window above the sink, watching the wind shake the trees.

"I know," I mutter. "And I'm sorry for the fallout."

"Sorry doesn't pay for the hours lost, the manpower shuffled, or the contract I had to renegotiate because one of my best went feral over his mate's heat."

I wince. Not because he's wrong. But because he's not exaggerating.

"I didn't go feral."

"You knocked Levi on his ass and abandoned the job."

"She was suffering, Dom."

The tremble of her voice, the raw panic laced in every breath.

She never said the word *help*, but I heard it anyway. I felt it in every muscle. My girl was drowning. And no job in the world comes before my mate.

Not now. Not ever.

The silence on the other end stretches, sharp as glass.

He knows. He's an Alpha. A decade older than me, blistered, and brittle around the edges, but he understands. He probably would've done the same if the old bastard would settle with a mate.

Finally, Rourke exhales like it pains him to agree.

"I don't ever want you to pull that shit again. If you've got a crisis, you fucking call me."

I grunt. "So, what now?"

"You're taking the next job. No excuses. No bailouts. You'll do it clean and by the book. You owe me that."

I grind my jaw. "Fine."

"Fine," he scoffs. "You don't even know what it is yet."

"Don't care. I'll do it."

Another pause, this one tighter.

"You've always been good, Blackwood. I don't want to lose you. Don't make me choose between the contract and the crisis next time."

The line goes dead before I can answer.

I toss the phone onto the counter. Rourke's voice still echoes in my skull like gravel under boots.

He's an old bastard and a pain in my ass, but he's not wrong. I left the team scrambling. Left the clients pissed.

I fucked up.

And yet... I'd do it again in a heartbeat.

But that doesn't mean I'm blind to the mess I left behind, out there and in here.

I rinse out the glass Rosie never touched, the one that sat half-full in front of her the entire time. Not a single sip. All because of her appointment today.

The water is warm, the sponge moving in slow, lazy circles, but my jaw's tight. Muscles wound like wire, tension licking across my shoulders like a storm rolling in. The frustration from this morning eating at me.

I should be there with her.

Not scrubbing glassware and pretending I'm not about to punch a damn hole in the wall.

She didn't want to eat.

Not unusual for her when she's nervous, but it still made something inside me twist.

She kept insisting she was fine. That she'd grab something later. But I'd seen the tremble in her hands when she opened the fridge. The way she stared at the food like it offended her.

So, I nudged her. Gently at first. Then again. And again.

"Just a few bites, sweetheart."

"You won't get through the appointment on an empty stomach."

"C'mon, for me?"

Eventually, she caved and ate a handful of fruit—small bites, like each one had to pass a test before it earned its place in her mouth.

She didn't look at me while she ate.

Didn't say much, either.

Only asked that I let her go to this appointment alone.

I wanted to deny her. I wanted to be there. To hear the confirmation from the doctor. To get all the gritty details that will keep Rosie and the baby healthy. But that damn plea in her eyes made it impossible to say no.

And that instant relief and soft smile on her face as she thanked me was a nice mirage before she crawled back inside herself.

She was like a shadow of the girl that usually greets me in the morning.

And I hated it.

Hated not being able to fix whatever was clawing at her. Hated that I couldn't just touch her and pull the fear out through her skin like a splinter.

I should've gone with her.

I rinse the glass, shaking the water off, and setting it down in the dish rack.

I look at the door. Waiting with bated breath for her to walk through it. And hopefully, this time with a smile.

For weeks now I've watched her recoil further into herself. Guilt and fear rearing their ugly head as she creates distance between us, inch by inch.

And I've let her.

I've watched it happen and filled the silence with touch. With kisses. With her name moaned into her neck like it was enough to tether her to me.

I thought if I loved her hard enough, fucked her soft enough, held her close enough…maybe all that fear would melt away.

I thought praise and pleasure could overwrite pain if I just gave her enough of it. Distracted her with enough of it.

But I should've known better.

Back in bed, the day we found out.

That flicker of guilt behind her eyes, right in the middle of my worship. I noticed it, and I didn't stop. I didn't ask.

I told myself it wasn't the time. Hell, it was time to celebrate. To fall into each other's arms with joy and… well…

Truth is, I was scared.

Scared if I asked, she'd say it was something I couldn't fix. Or more accurately, something I wouldn't want to fix.

That this fragile joy we'd found would crack down the middle.

That she'd say she was still broken. Or worse, that she didn't want this. And so I tried to will it away with blind lust.

But that's not love. Not the kind I promised her.

So now the plan has changed. Now, when she walks through that door, I'm not going to just hold her.

I'm going to listen.

To every word. Even if it's the very thing I'm most scared of.

If there's something eating at her, I'll dig until I find it.

If she needs space, I'll give it.

If she needs my voice, my hands, my whole damn heart, it's hers. Every damn piece of it.

Whatever she needs, I'll try to be that, without avoiding it like the coward I've been.

No more hoping sex and sweetness will be enough to hide the cracks.

I'm her Alpha, and it's time I fucking act like it.

CHAPTER 15
ROSIE

The door clicks shut behind me, and for the first time in weeks, I don't feel like I'm holding my breath.

It's still there, of course, the fear. The nerves. The possibility that something could go wrong. But it doesn't own me the way it did when I left this morning.

The in-office test was positive.

The ultrasound is booked. My blood draw went smoothly.

I am pregnant. *Really* pregnant. And it's no longer just a line on a stick in my bathroom. It's real and it's all ours.

My chest feels lighter. My heart warmer. I'm still scared, but underneath it all, there's this quiet hum of joy. And I want to relish in it with my mate. My Theron.

I want to tell him everything. Share every small insignificant detail of the appointment and just fall into his arms, breathe in his scent, and feel the weight of his praise pressed into my skin like sunlight.

I slip off my shoes and drop my bag by the door.

"Alpha?" I call softly, already smiling.

But there's no response.

I step further into the house, just about to call out again, until I freeze.

Theron is sitting at the small dining table, his massive arms braced against the wood, fingers laced together. He doesn't look up right away. He doesn't move.

His brows are low. Jaw tense. That little muscle in his cheek jumping like it always does when he's holding something in.

He looks…angry. Or at least close to it.

My smile falters, confusion cracking through the warmth in my chest. "Theron?"

His eyes lift, meeting mine and I feel exposed. Like he's not just looking at me. He's looking *through* me.

A shiver creeps up the back of my neck. I wrap my arms around myself, suddenly unsure if it's the air that turned cold or just me.

"Sit. Now." His tone is sharp.

I sit before I even realize I've moved. My hands are trembling now, twisting the fabric of my skirt, and all that warmth I brought in with me is bleeding out through the soles of my feet.

I sit beside him, my eyes flicking toward his before dropping fast. The silence between us is loud, louder than it should be. Like the whole house is holding its breath.

I don't know what I've done wrong, but the air between us feels like it's about to split open.

"Look at me." His voice is low. Not rough. Not cruel. But it cuts through the air like a knife. I sheepishly raise my gaze and when our eyes meet, I wish they hadn't.

Because there's no anger there. There's only hurt and worry.

"Whatever you're about to say," I whisper, "can you please just—"

"No," he interrupts, voice still calm, but commanding. "I want the truth, Rose. And you are going to give it to me."

I blink. My throat tightens at the sound of my name. He always calls me 'Rosie'.

"No lies. No half-answers. No pretending you're okay." His voice doesn't rise, but it vibrates with deep emotion. Like the rumbling before an eruption.

"Talk to me. Please."

I'm silent. I don't know what to say. What to share, what to avoid.

He leans in, elbows on the table, and that wild green gaze pins me in place.

"You've been distant for weeks," he says. "You flinch when I touch you. You won't meet my eyes. You avoid food. And this morning, you were like a damn ghost." His voice cracks.

"And I didn't push. I didn't want to scare you. But I can't... I can't keep pretending I don't notice. I see you slipping away from me, and I don't know how to stop it."

I inhale, but he keeps going.

"You're pregnant," he says, softer now. "And you barely say the word." He swallows, jaw tight.

"So I need to ask you something. And I need you to answer me with the truth, Rose." His hand slides across the table, stopping just short of mine.

"Do you want this?" He pauses, the silence cutting deep. "A baby. With me."

I'm stunned. Speechless. Utterly and completely heartbroken.

How can he ask that?

How can he look at me and ask that? He knows. He was there. He saw the way I fell apart after every single negative test. He held me after every appointment that made me question my status as an Omega.

I was scared but now I'm angry.

Furious.

At him for asking that insane question. And at myself, for making him feel the need to.

Because this is my fault too.

I let shame speak louder than truth. I let doubt build a wall so high, even he couldn't see over it. And now I've been carrying this life inside me with resentment. With fear so profound it drowned out my joy.

God, I did this.

My mouth opens, but I can't speak. A sob bursts out instead, broken and too loud for the quiet room.

My hands fly to my face as the tears come hard, hot, and unforgiving. My shoulders shake, my breath catches, and it feels like I'm unraveling from the inside out.

A war rages inside me, blistering, breath-stealing fury clashing against a soul-crushing ice-cold sadness. And underneath it all is just this ache.

I don't know who I'm more angry at. Him or me. Because I let the silence grow between us. I let fear take the wheel.

Now I'm standing in the wreckage of something we were supposed to celebrate, and I can't tell if I want to scream, collapse, or pull him into my arms and beg him to forgive me for everything I didn't say.

Theron's chair scrapes against the floor, turning to face me better. He watches me with eyes full of pain I didn't see until now.

"Rosie…" he says gently, like my name alone is a prayer he doesn't know how to finish. "I would never force this. I would never…it's your body. Your choice."

His voice breaks, and I watch, as tears begin to fall down his face. "But if you don't want this. If you couldn't…" He swallows, his Adam's apple bobbing in his throat, his chest rising with a shaky breath.

"I'd still stay. I'd still be yours. No matter what. No matter how it hurts," he cries, choking on his words. "Because I chose you. I'll always choose you."

God.

My heart twists painfully in my chest.

This dumb, beautiful Alpha, is crying, breaking apart over something I never even said. Jumping to conclusions I never wanted him to reach.

"I'm sorry," I choke out, voice raw. "I'm so sorry, Theron."

My chest heaves, my shoulders shake uncontrollably. "But fuck you."

"Sweetheart…" He tries to soothe me, to calm me but God it only hurts more.

I wipe at my cheeks, blinking hard. "Yes! Yes, I want this. A baby. With you. You, stupid, stupid Alpha!" I shout, my anger seemingly winning its war. "God, you should know! You should know this better than anyone, you absolute ass!"

My voice cracks. "But I couldn't say it out loud. Because I was scared. After everything. I was too scared." I hang my head in shame.

"Scared of what, Rosie?" He asks with such sweetness I almost want to slap him, and he kneels beside me, leaving behind his chair.

"That if I let myself believe it, really believe it…it'd be ripped away from me. From us. And I…I couldn't face that."

I press my palm to my belly and Theron places his upon mine and my anger simmers. Swelling love in my heart stealing its heat.

"I've been holding my breath since the test turned positive. Like any moment, I'd feel it all vanish. Like it wasn't mine to keep."

I lift my gaze, finally meeting his. "And I didn't want you to see that. I didn't want to ruin your joy with all my crazy doubt." Another sob hits, quieter this time.

"But don't you ever assume I don't want this baby. I never, never, want to hear you say that again." I break down, falling forward and crying into his crouched form.

"Never." He repeats, making a promise.

I don't know how long he lets me cry like that, maybe a few seconds, maybe minutes. All I know is that when the tears slow and my lungs stop shaking, I feel him move, standing tall once again.

His arms slide under my thighs and back, lifting me from the chair like I weigh nothing at all. He settles into the chair I originally sat on, placing me onto his lap.

One arm wraps tight around my waist. The other cradles the back of my head, guiding me to rest against his chest. His scent is all around me, warm and familiar and comfortingly safe.

For a moment, he just holds me.

And then his voice, soft and slightly rough, breaks the silence once more.

"This is my fault too, sweetheart."

I blink, my cheek pressed to his shirt.

"I kept dragging you back into bed, thinking if I kissed you enough, touched you enough…that whatever was tearing you apart would just go quiet." His hand strokes along my spine, lulling me into a sense of calm.

"I saw you hurting. I saw the fear. And I ignored it."

His voice dips lower, rasping against my ear and I bury my face against his chest, clinging to the warmth of his voice and the tremble in it.

"Because I was scared too."

I shift against him, but his arms tighten, like letting go isn't an option.

"I was so damn happy when that test read positive. I let myself believe it without question. And when I saw that flicker behind your eyes, I told myself it didn't matter. That if I just loved you harder, louder…it'd be enough." He breathes deep.

"I really thought you didn't want this."

"Theron." I try to warn him not to say any more. I don't want to hear this.

"Please, I know I promised but I need to say this. Please Rosie." His palm flattens over my belly again, his touch gentle. With reluctance I let him speak. "I was selfish enough to think I could make you want it." His voice breaks, emotion tight in his throat again.

"I should've asked. I should've held space for you, not just held your body. And I'm sorry for that."

We both should have done a lot of things differently. But would that have changed anything?

If he had asked, would I have been honest? If I had spoken up, would he have truly understood?

I don't know. And the truth is, we can't go back.

We can't rewrite the silence or the shame or the things we were too scared to say or do. All we can do now is choose what comes next.

CHAPTER 16
THERON

She's curled into my lap face pressed to my chest and we share this time to calm our emotions. To just breathe and settle.

My hand moves slowly across her back, up and down in steady passes. Calming. Reassuring. Repeating the same silent promise over and over.

She's quieter now. Her breathing deeper. But I can still feel the tremor in her body, like her mind is still thinking, running circles around itself with questions, concerns and a multitude of answers that don't need to be given.

I have so much regret. For not asking sooner. For making assumptions that just pissed her off. For every misstep I made these last few weeks.

I rest my chin against the top of her head, breathing her in. She smells like vanilla and sugar. *Sweet.* My sweet Omega.

"I'm sorry," she whispers again, so softly, but there's strength behind it. "We can't change what happened, and I'm sorry for my part in this."

I shake my head. "No more apologies, sweetheart. We both missed the mark."

"We did. But we don't have to focus on that. We just need to be better. For each other." She shifts just enough to look up at me, her eyes swollen from crying but clearer somehow. Steadier.

"I want to tell you about the appointment," she says sheepishly, a little smile cracking on her face.

"Yeah?"

She nods, fingers tightening in the fabric of my shirt. "It was—" she hesitates, "good. Better than I thought it would be at least."

Her smile brightens as she says "I'm due November 12th."

"November 12th," I parrot back. A little over seven months away.

She nods but her smile dims by a fraction as she goes on about the appointment. "They ran tests, gave me a list of supplements. I'm scheduled for an ultrasound in two weeks."

Something in my chest lifts. Excitement. "That's soon."

"Yeah." A small smile pulls at her lips. "I thought it would terrify me, but it didn't. Not completely."

I brush my knuckles across her cheek, and she leans into it.

"I'm still scared," she admits. "I think I will be for…" She huffs. "Forever and a day."

She pauses, her eyes searching mine. "But I can't carry it alone. I can't."

I nod slowly. "You won't have to."

"And that goes for you too," she adds. "No more assuming. No more hiding behind kisses and bed sheets. If something's wrong…you tell me."

I let out a slow breath, pressing my forehead to hers.

"Deal."

She exhales, but I feel the tension still knotted in her shoulders. There's more. I can feel it moving under her skin. Her mind still clouded with unspoken concern.

"There's something else," I say gently. "Isn't there?"

Her lips part. And this time, she doesn't hide.

"Dr. Bryant said…" she swallows, "she said being thirty and…obese puts me at higher risk. That there could be complications." She says it without bitterness. Just a plain and simple fact.

"I know she wasn't cruel," she adds. "She was just honest."

"Rosie—"

"I know," she cuts in with a sigh interrupting my incoming rant.

With a tender smile on her lips, she continues saying, "I know you love me. You worship me like I'm a damn holy relic."

Damn right.

She lifts her hand, touches my chest over my heart.

"But that's not what I need right now."

"Okay." I kiss her temple and give her the space she needs.

"It's not about how I *look*. It's about what I *don't know*. I don't know if something's going to go wrong. I don't know if my body can handle this. I don't know if I'll get to hold this baby. I don't know if…" Her voice falters. "If I'll survive it, if it does go wrong."

The words land like stone in my gut, cold and heavy, impossible to move. I want to deny them, to promise her nothing will ever go wrong. But I can't. And she doesn't need empty promises or vows about things that aren't in my control.

"And that's what terrifies me," she finishes, speaking so softly it's less of a whisper and more like a breath. "That I'll let you hope, and dream, and fall in love with something, and then my body will betray us both."

She closes her eyes like she's ashamed of that very real possible nightmare.

I wrap my arms tighter around her, anchoring her to me, pressing my lips to her temple once more.

"You're not alone," I whisper. "You won't ever be alone in this."

She doesn't need absolutes or impossible promises. She needs to be heard. She needs comfort and for her Alpha, for me, to stop hiding behind strength and be present with her, even in this realm of unknowns we find ourselves in.

She exhales slowly against my chest, her fingers still curled into my shirt like she's afraid to let go.

But there's something different in the air now. The pressure has shifted. The storm has passed.

Not completely, maybe. But enough. Enough for both of us to breathe.

"I love you," I murmur into her hair.

"I know," she says, soft and certain.

And just like that, the earth settles beneath us again.

I hold her tighter, one hand drifting slowly up her back. I think about everything we've said, everything we finally let out into the open and how much easier it feels to breathe. To be *here*, with her.

She opened up. I listened. We let ourselves bleed a little. And we're better for it.

For once, I didn't try to fix her. I just held the pieces while she put us back together and made us all the stronger.

CHAPTER 17
ROSIE

The waiting room smells like lemon cleaner and too much anxiety.

But this time, it's not just *my* anxiety clogging my senses.

Theron's hand is wrapped around mine, thumb tracing slow circles over my knuckles. I don't know if he's doing it to calm me or himself, but either way, it works.

"Still okay?" he asks, voice low and warm as his fingers tighten gently around mine.

He's been doing that a lot lately. Checking in. Watching me a little closer. Making sure I'm not hiding behind a practiced smile or a cracked mask.

And I'd be lying if I said it didn't get on my nerves sometimes.

Every time he thinks he sees something in my eyes, a flicker of doubt, a shadow of fear, he's asking. Offering me space to speak. Space to fall apart, if I need to. And avoiding stupid conclusions too.

He never rushes me. Never pushes.

He's not trying to fix it, just hold it. Carry whatever I hand him without flinching.

Even when it's something ridiculous. Like the fact that we ran out of cream cheese this morning and I nearly cried like a child finding out Santa Clause or the Tooth Fairy aren't real.

I glance at him, this man who drives me crazy in the best and worst of ways, and nod.

"I'm okay," I say. "A little nervous. But mostly excited."

His lips tug into a soft smile. "Excited is good."

He presses a kiss to my temple, and I lean into his warmth just as the nurse calls my name. My stomach tightens, but when I look up at Theron, he's already standing.

He reaches for my hand without a word, his grip firm and steady.

As we follow the nurse toward the back, he stays just a step ahead of me, like his body is already bracing to shield me from whatever's coming.

My hero.

The nurse is sweet but efficient, guiding us through the hallway with a practiced smile and soft instructions.

"Room four," she says, holding the door open with a practiced smile. "Go ahead and remove everything from the waist down, including underwear. You can leave your bra on. There's a gown and a drape on the chair. Just have a seat on the table when you're ready. The tech will be in shortly."

Theron squeezes my hand and follows me in like I might disappear if he lets go. The door falls closed and with it, the nurse leaves us alone in the room.

The exam table takes up most of the space, with a mounted monitor on the wall and a second screen positioned where the tech can guide the wand and watch everything in real time. There's a small cart with equipment beside it, and a rolling stool tucked neatly into the corner.

I glance at Theron.

He's watching me, but not in the way he usually does. There's no heat in his gaze, no teasing smirk, no slow look down my body.

Just focused silence.

Just him seeing me, and all the nerves I'm trying to hide under layers of bad pep-talks and breath control.

I reach for the gown and start untying the small shoestring-like ties of my skirt, but he steps forward without a word.

"Let me," he says softly.

I hesitate for a moment, then allow him to help me.

He kneels, not rushing or fumbling, like a nervous man might. His fingers skim the waistband of my skirt, tugging the fabric down carefully.

There's no commentary. No heat. No wink or grin.

Just the soft whisper of cloth sliding down my hips, the quiet thump of it hitting the floor, and his hands keeping steady as I step out.

I drape the gown over my shoulder, arms threading through the stiff sleeves. It's hospital standard. Thin cotton, soft with wear, and absolutely too small for me.

The ties barely graze one another across my belly. They never stood a chance. I try to pull the fabric tighter, try to cover more of my belly, but there's just too much of me and not enough gown.

I glance down, cheeks heating. The gap across my midsection gapes open like it's mocking me. This isn't because I'm pregnant. It's because

I'm fat, or 'obese' as the damn paperwork likes to say.

Theron says nothing.

Instead, he gently sets a hand at the small of my back and helps guide me onto the table. Like none of it, the gown, the exposure, the bare vulnerability, matters to him.

He reaches for the drape, unfolding it with care, and lays it across my lap with deliberate tenderness. It covers me to the knees, modest and neat, like he's tucking me in before a storm.

And still, not a single crude comment. No hand lingering on my thigh. No raised brow. Nothing.

Just silence. And it's a little unnerving.

He meets my gaze again, and this time, I finally notice it.

He's scared too.

Not of me. Not of the gown or the room or the nurse who's about to come back.

But of what we might see, or not see, on that threatening monitor.

"You're scared." I whisper the words, like I'm not sure I believe it myself.

He doesn't flinch. Doesn't deny it. Just takes a breath, like he's deciding how honest to be.

"Yeah," he says, voice quiet. "I am."

I blink, surprised by the weight of it. How he says it so simply, without shame.

"I keep thinking I'm supposed to be the one holding it all together," he goes on, eyes fixed on the space between us. "I'm supposed to be the strong Alpha. Not a man terrified of…I'm not even sure what exactly."

His hand tightens around mine, not too much, just enough that I feel the tension there. The restraint.

"But I've never been this scared of silence before." He glances at the monitor and my gaze follows. That damn screen will either show us our new world or destroy it.

"Of waiting for something to appear. Of hearing nothing where there should be a heartbeat." My throat goes tight.

"I didn't want to tell you," he says, softer now. "Didn't want my fear to make yours worse. So, I've been trying to stay calm." He finally looks at me.

"But when you're lying there…small and quiet and trying to breathe through it." He swallows hard. "I don't want to be strong. I just want to protect you. And I don't know if I can."

I reach for his face, fingers brushing over his jaw. He leans into it without hesitation.

"You are protecting me," I say. "Right now. Just by being here."

His eyes close, dark lashes resting against his cheeks, and when he exhales, it's like something inside him lets go.

A loud knock interrupts us suddenly.

"Ultrasound tech!" comes the too-cheerful voice from the other side of the door. "Ready when you are!"

Theron kisses the back of my hand. Then he lets go and settles back in his chair. Ready to confront whatever might be revealed on the screen.

CHAPTER 18
ROSIE

The door swings open revealing a much too cheerful woman.

"Hi there!" chirps with a sickeningly sweet voice. "I'm Sadie and I'll be doing your ultrasound today!"

She's younger than I expected. Pretty, too. Not in a threatening way, exactly, just that fresh-faced, wide-eyed young kind of pretty that makes you think she's never had a truly bad day in her life.

She almost skips into the room. This girl obviously loves this job, and the way she beams as she sits on the stool in front of the machine beside the bed feels out of place, like it doesn't match the weight in my chest or the silence that's just barely holding me together.

And then she sees Theron. I watch her eyes dip, widen, flick back up to his face—and suddenly, there are hearts in her eyes.

"Oh! You must be dad," she says, voice already softening, with an awkward sultriness. "Welcome."

Theron doesn't move. Just nods. "Thanks."

Her smile grows so big it could light the whole dang room.

I roll my eyes and look away. This is just what I needed, a young, giddy girl throwing heart-eyes at my mate on top of the rest of the bullshit I'm feeling today.

She's probably an Omega too. Most likely on suppressants, that's the only reason I can't catch her scent.

Sadie hums as she loads the machine, chatting a little too casually for someone with this much anxiety permeating the room.

"Gotta say," she starts brightly, snapping on a glove, "it's always nice seeing couples like you two come in. The way you're holding hands… that doesn't happen as often as you'd think."

I manage a polite smile. Barely.

"I swear, sometimes it's like pulling teeth just to get the dads to show up, let alone sit still and care!"

She glances at Theron with something dangerously close to a dreamy sigh. "But not you. You're like…here. It's rare. And really sweet. Which I appreciate."

She *appreciates*? I'm sorry did she forget I'm the pregnant mate?

Theron doesn't respond. Thank God.

"I mean…" she continues, smoothing the material of her pink scrubs, "when I imagine my own mate, I hope they're someone big. And Protective. And perfect just for me."

Another not-so-subtle glance his way.

"Maybe they'll be just as… Hearty as you."

I blink.

Hearty? Who says that?

Theron clears his throat, loudly, and gestures to the monitor. "We ready?"

Sadie blinks, like she forgot why we're here at all. "Oh! Right! Sorry, yes, we're all set."

She taps quickly on keys of the machine and that once lustful tone is replaced with one I can tolerate a whole lot more.

"We'll be looking for placement first," she says, cheerfully. "Then size and viability. We should also be able to hear a nice strong heartbeat today."

I nod tightly, trying to smile back, but it doesn't reach anything beneath my skin.

Sadie preps the wand and the gel like this is just another Tuesday. Like my world doesn't hinge on what we're about to see.

Anxiety grips my heart, and I almost feel like I can't breathe, but Theron squeezes my hand once, gently. His thumb traces circles again, that same steady rhythm he always gives me when I can't find my own.

Sadie moves closer.

"Alright, go ahead and lower the sheet and open. Oh! Gown's already open, perfect!"

I suppose that's her chipper way of saying this gown doesn't fit me either. Lovely.

"Okay, I'm going to apply the gel now. It'll feel a little cold."

I close my eyes, exhale hard through my nose.

Fear swells. Not panic like before, just a sharp ache under my ribs, like my body is bracing to break.

The gel hits my skin, slick and icy against the curve of my lower belly. I flinch.

"Sorry," Sadie says, the smallest bit of remorse behind her words.

She positions the wand and presses down. Small taps on the keyboard grate on my already frayed nerves.

I don't breathe.

"Where are you baby?" Sadie asks, moving the wand and pressing hard into me.

She can't find you.

Panic starts to race inside my chest and the silence grows teeth. I grip Theron's hand like it's the only thing anchoring me to this table.

Theron's hand squeezes mine, almost too tightly, as he too searches for any comfort at the long search for the baby inside me.

"Ah ha! Found you, little troublemaker."

My eyes snap open and there you are.

A flickering blur. A shape barely formed. And yet the most incredible thing I've ever seen.

Sadie says something, maybe a measurement or a number, but I don't hear it. All I pay any attention to is the little blob on screen and the relief washing through me.

The air feels still, reverent, like the room is holding its breath right along with us. That flickering shape on the screen, tiny, shifting, real, roots me in place, and at the same time, lifts something heavy out of my chest.

I feel his thumb sweep across my knuckles and I turn my head to meet his eyes, but his are glued to the screen. A wide silly insanely happy proud smile plastered on his face.

That look is what I've been waiting for. This moment where I see a clear beautiful sign that our dream is becoming a reality.

Sadie clears her throat, the cheerful edge softened just slightly now.

"Would you two…" she pauses, her voice gentler, "like to hear the heartbeat?"

"Yes," Theron says in rushed excitement.

He leans forward slightly, his gaze still fixed on the screen, like if he blinks, the image might vanish. Like if he lets go of this moment, he'll never get it back.

"Please," he adds, quieter this time.

Sadie's smile softens, no coyness now. Just warmth as she taps a few keys on the machine.

Ba-dump.

Ba-dump. Ba-dump. Ba-dump.

The room fills with the sound of life. It's quick, and strong, and so beautifully loud.

My breath hitches. My heart stumbles.

That sound.

It's not just a heartbeat. It's your heartbeat.

I feel Theron's hand move again, gripping tighter, grounding me. The overwhelming emotion of love in his eyes as he looks at me causes those tears I'd been holding off to finally spill.

But from relief. I didn't even realize how scared I'd been, until the fear let go of me.

The sound fades from the speakers, but it echoes in my chest, like it left a mark inside me.

Sadie's voice is gentler now, watching the scene before her.

"I'll give you two a moment," she says softly. "But before I go…"

She grabs a towel from the counter and wipes away most of the gel from my belly, her touch surprisingly delicate now.

"You can get dressed when you're ready," she adds. "And then just check in with the receptionist at the front desk, we'll get you on the books for your twenty-week scan."

I nod, still unable to speak. My gaze stuck on the face of my Alpha.

She steps back, wheels her stool under the machine, and gives one last look, this one free of the earlier flirtation.

"Congratulations," she says, and then slips out, leaving the door to whisper shut behind her.

Silence settles over the room again, but this time, it's golden. Safe.

Theron leans in and brushes a tear from my cheek with the back of his fingers, his expression caught somewhere between awe and hunger.

"You okay?" he murmurs.

I nod. Still teary. Still smiling. "They're real. It's all real."

"Yeah, baby they're real...and strong. Just like their mama." He brushes another stray tear from my face. "I could hear it in their heartbeat."

The heartbeat. It still echoes in my head. "It was strong, wasn't it?"

He leans down, kisses the corner of my mouth, then my jaw, then my temple. "We're really doing this, Rosie. We're having a baby."

The fear I woke with, and have been haunted by for weeks, still lingers but it's eclipsed at this moment by something bigger and brighter.

Raw, breathtaking happiness.

"Let's go home," Theron smiles, but his voice carries a dangerous tone as he continues and whispers, "And the second we do get home, I'm going to devour you."

An almost goofy laugh escapes me. "You're insane," I say with a slap to his chest, struggling to get off the exam table.

He grins. "Only for you."

CHAPTER 19
THERON

The second the front door closes shut behind us, I'm on her.

My hand slides into her hair, and her back hits the wall with a soft gasp that rips through me like a prayer answered. She looks up at me, flushed, still a little teary, and fucking perfect.

All I want is to fall to my knees and worship her.

"You heard it," I whisper, voice already wrecked with emotion. "Tell me you heard it, Rosie."

Her breath stutters. "I did."

That sound. That heartbeat.

Our baby.

Our child.

Living inside my mate.

I dip down and kiss her like it'll never be enough. Like I'm trying to press every promise into her mouth.

"You're carrying our baby," I murmur against her lips. "Do you even know what that does to me?"

She shivers.

"You walked out of that room glowing, sweetheart. And all I could think about was putting you on your back."

My palms worship every soft, full curve like I'm carving her into memory. "My Omega," I groan, dragging my mouth down her throat. "My sweet, beautiful mate."

I try to flip her skirt but the damn thing fights me, making me look like a fumbling fool for a moment. Whoever said skirts were easy access fucking lied.

"Help me baby, I want to worship you the way you deserve to be."

With assistance, she strips—her skirt first, then her plain grey t-shirt, leaving her in just a mixed-matched bra and panties set.

I hum into her throat, the scent of her arousal causing a possessive growl to escape me, and I sink to my knees, not just because I want her, but because I need to honor the body carrying my whole damn world.

I drag her panties down, not wasting time, and press my lips to her pussy.

"You were made to be worshipped," I growl, tongue sliding against her. "To be filled. To be loved."

She whimpers, hips twitching like the words alone unravel her, legs shaking and yet, I've barely started.

"By me," I growl, licking a slow, taunting stripe over her clit. "Only me, my sweet Omega."

I devour her like she's the only thing keeping me alive, my tongue strokes deep, slow, filthy circles against her clit while I slip one of my fingers into her soaked pussy, then another. Her cunt clenches around them as I curl them inside her.

She arches against the wall, thighs trembling, breath catching.

"Going to come for me, Rosie?" I murmur against her wet heat, my voice thick with reverence and sin. "Want to fall apart for me, my good girl?"

She nods, breathy moans of *yes* repeat like a mantra.

And to her utter disappointment, I stop, pulling my fingers from her begging pussy and press a sympathetic kiss to her mound.

She groans in frustration, hips chasing me. "Don't tease me," she scolds.

I stand wiping my mouth and kiss her with deep passion, savoring her taste on my lips.

"You'll come," I promise, voice rough with hunger. "But not here."

I grip her hips and lift her. Her short legs struggle to wrap around my waist and her nails dig into my shoulders.

"I want you in our bed," I growl against her ear. "Not in a doorway like a couple of college brats trying to get a quickie in before class."

I carry her down the hallway, her breath stuttering against my neck, her body throbbing with everything I didn't let her have.

"I want to praise you, Rosie," I whisper. "I want to savor every moment as I fuck you so full and hard, you'll feel me for days.

I nudge the bedroom door open with my foot.

"And when you finally come…" I lay her down, eyes locking on the most devastatingly beautiful woman I've ever known. "It'll be with my knot locked inside you and my seed leaking down your thighs."

I undress quickly, stripping off the layers of clothes like the final challenge before my grand feast.

I crawl up the bed, over her trembling form.

"I'll fill you," I vow, dragging my cock along her weeping cunt, rubbing between her folds and letting the wetness gather along it. "Again. And again."

I press my forehead to hers.

"I'm going to give you everything, Rosie. This baby is just the start. I'm going to breed you so full, and so often, you'll never have a day without my cum dripping out of you."

She writhes under me, already half gone, already aching for it. And God, I haven't even given her what she needs yet.

"You want that, don't you, Omega? To stay full of me? Of our babies?"

She gasps, wide-eyed and wild.

"Yes!" she cries out, voice cracking with desperate need and more than a little irritation.

I slam into her with a groan that's more beast than man, burying myself in one hard, brutal thrust—a cruelly kind reward for her honesty

She screams, hands flying to my shoulders, her nails dragging down my back in perfect, burning lines.

"Fuck," I growl, pumping into her, hard and fast and punishing.

"God," I pant, thrusting deep. "You take me so damn well. Tight little cunt made to be fucked."

She whimpers beneath me, hips arching to meet every stroke, her legs locking around me like she's trying to keep me inside her forever. Like I'd want to be anywhere else than buried between her voluptuous thighs.

Her walls flutter and squeeze around my cock, slick and welcoming, and it's driving me feral. I sink my teeth into the sweet spot where her neck meets her shoulder.

She herself turns a little feral, and her mouth finds my throat and bites back.

The second her teeth sink in, her pussy clamps down like a vice, and I feel her come hard, her whole body wracked with it, legs trembling, voice breaking as she moans my name over and over and over.

And I am right behind her. My knot swells thick, locking us together with one final, ruthless thrust that makes her arch and sob through another wave.

And I spill into her. Pulse after pulse of thick, coating heat flooding her until she's shaking under me, knotted and pregnant and radiant.

Her cunt clenches with every spurt, coaxing every drop from me, her body greedy for it, perfect for it.

We stay like that for a while, tangled and breathless, skin slick, her body trembling in the sweetest aftershocks while my knot keeps us locked together. Claimed and bound.

She's still gasping, her head thrown back, lips parted like she doesn't quite remember how to breathe.

I kiss her temple, then her jaw, then the curve of her shoulder. Like I'm giving thanks for something I'll never deserve enough.

"C'mere," I murmur, shifting above her.

She whines as I move, the knot tugging uncomfortably, so I roll us gently, forcing her on top, cradling her to my chest with both arms wrapped tight around her back. She melts into me, cheek pressed to my heart, breath still unsteady against my skin.

"There," I whisper. "That's better."

She hums a song softly, a melody I don't recognize while her fingers dance across my skin. I drag my hand down her spine, anchoring us both in the afterglow.

"You're everything to me," I say into her hair. "You know that, right?"

She doesn't respond, just continues to hum her quiet tune.

"I could've had a thousand different lives," I murmur, voice thick. "But none of them would've meant shit without you."

I kiss her forehead, petting her hair and staring with wonder. And she just lays there, full of me, tied to me, and I swear the world has never been more perfect than it is right now.

"I love you and this life, with you, Theron."

Damn.

I stand corrected.

Now, the world is perfect.

CHAPTER 20
ROSIE

The scent of strawberry milk and pen ink has become my new comfort. Every day I concoct my mixture of sugary strawberry syrup and whole milk and sit down to plan out a small but grand baby shower we will host in October, with a special Halloween flare.

And while I plan, Theron paces the living room behind me, fighting to keep his anger in check while trying to schedule house tours around my cravings and OB visits.

Today is really no different. I sit on the couch, my strawberry milk already half gone as I lick envelopes and watch a documentary about the Greenbrier Ghost.

"No, earlier would be better," Theron says into the phone, his tone clipped but polite. "She gets tired in the afternoons. We'd like to see the house before noon if possible."

I smile and shake my head, sealing another envelope in our stack of baby shower invitations with a firm press of my thumb. The glittery "You're Invited!" sticker winks up at me like this whole thing is real now. It is real.

I can't believe I'm already twenty-three weeks along. Just a little over halfway.

And so far?

Bliss.

My monthly checkups with Dr. Bryant have gone beautifully. No complications. No red flags. Just the normal poking and prodding and the occasional *are you drinking enough water?* lecture.

She asked if we wanted to know the gender at our twelve-week appointment, and although my reaction was a bit harsher than I intended, I didn't want her to blurt out the results.

I've always dreamed of that moment, when the doctor places my baby on my chest and smiles, saying, "It's a little girl," or maybe a boy. It doesn't matter. Not really. As long as they're healthy. As long as they're here.

I want to feel it. That shift. That moment where everything changes. Where I look into their eyes and just… know.

They're mine.

Theron didn't argue. He never does. Just agreed with a sweet, "Whatever you want, baby."

Our second ultrasound was magical, even despite Sadie, the overly friendly tech, using the appointment as an excuse to gab about the matchmaker she hired to find her an Alpha "as hearty as yours." I nearly choked on my juice box.

To Theron's credit, he didn't even flinch. Just smiled and kept his focus right where it belonged. On the flickering, perfect little profile on the monitor.

The last couple months have been damn near perfect. Strange, given how the rest of our lives usually go. But since that first ultrasound, everything's felt…settled.

Theron hasn't been able to keep his hands to himself, which, frankly, I haven't minded. Especially not with the way my belly's started to swell. It's like every inch I grow only makes him fall harder. He watches me like I've hung the moon. Like I'm divine.

And oddly enough, for once in my life, I feel like I am.

I thought I'd feel self-conscious, like most women do when they start buying clothes three sizes bigger than usual. But I've always been fat. My body has always shifted and stretched to fit life as it comes. So no, the size doesn't faze me. I'd happily be the size of a house if it meant I'd get to hold my baby just a little sooner.

Theron finally ends the call with a sigh and drops onto the couch beside me like gravity finally caught up with him.

He leans his head back, eyes closed, one arm thrown dramatically across the back of the cushions.

"That was way more complicated than it needed to be," he mutters.

I smirk, "Did they try to schedule us for a seven o'clock showing again?"

He cracks one eye open to glare at me, affectionate and exasperated. "Eight thirty. But I talked them down. We're set for nine a.m. tomorrow." His expression softens as he watches me press the last baby shower invitation into the envelope stack. "I think this one might be it, Rosie."

I raise a brow. "The one?"

He nods, quieter now. "It's not perfect yet. But I think I could make it that way. For us. For them." His eyes drift to my belly.

Without thinking, his hand slides across the space between us and settles over my middle. Warm. Solid. So familiar now that I don't even flinch the way I used to—back when my head was clouded with doubt and his touch felt more like a distraction than comfort. Now, I just lean into him and let out a soft sigh.

The baby kicks. A small, firm flutter beneath his palm.

We both freeze.

Then Theron's entire face lights up like its Christmas morning and I just handed him a positive test all over again.

"I'm sorry, did you want to be part of the conversation too, my angel?" he whispers, eyes wide with wonder like this is the first time we've ever felt the baby wiggle inside me.

I nod, smiling, heart swelling all over again.

His hand presses a little firmer, protective and awed.

"They're saying hi," I mutter. "Hi, mommy. Hi, daddy." I laugh.

"Our baby is excited for a freshly painted bedroom stuffed to the ceiling with toys." Another kick, and Theron's smile grows wider.

"You're such a sap."

"Damn right I am."

We sit like that for a long while, just staring in awe at my belly. His hand following every motion the baby makes inside of me.

Then his phone rings loudly against the armrest with all the subtlety of a foghorn. Theron groans like he's been personally insulted by the ringtone and reluctantly drags his hand away from me to check the screen.

Theron sighs, glancing at the screen, then he sits up straighter, shoulders tensing.

"Rourke," he mutters.

I frown. "Your boss?"

He nods, already answering the phone before I can say more.

"This is Blackwood." His voice shifts, professional, clipped.

I watch him as he listens, jaw ticking, his free hand curling into a loose fist against his thigh. Whatever's being said, it's not good. Or at least, not simple.

"Yeah, I'm cleared," he says after a pause. "I can travel."

My chest tightens.

Travel?

He looks at me then, just a glance, but it's enough that I know exactly what he's feeling. The guilt. The hesitation. The promise he knows he's about to break.

I go still, baby shower invitations forgotten.

"Mhm. Tomorrow?" He scrubs a hand down his face. "Can I have an hour to call you back? I need to check some things."

Another pause. Then, "Thanks. I'll be in touch."

He hangs up and stares at the phone like it might solve the problem for him if he just glares hard enough.

I clear my throat, voice low. "A job?"

Typically, Theron works from home or out of the main office just outside of town. But if they're calling about a job, it means a security detail—miles away from me. Just like when my heat started a few months ago.

Theron nods slowly. "One of our teams dropped last-minute. Low-risk cargo run through Colorado wilderness. They need a lead."

"And you said you're cleared to travel."

His eyes meet mine, remorseful. "It's only a few days."

I look down at the soft swell of my stomach. The spot where Theron's hand had just been. Where our baby had just kicked.

"A few days," I echo, quieter now.

He nods, watching me carefully.

And for a second, I'm not on the couch. I'm in our bedroom. Wrapped in blankets, sweat-drenched and shaking, my body tearing itself apart while I cried out into an empty room, while my Alpha was miles away, and I was curled into a nest of pain, begging for him with no one to hear me.

My body still remembers the ache, even if the burn faded long ago—gone since the start of my pregnancy. What lingers is the hollow weight of an empty house. The memory of screaming into a pillow, crying his name until my throat was raw.

"What if I don't want you to go? What if I ask, no, beg you stay?" I avoid his eyes, my hand drifting instinctively over my bump. The baby shifting beneath my palm.

"It won't be like last time, Rosie, I have to work. We want to buy a house, baby." He slides closer, cupping my face with both hands, but not forcing me to face his gaze.

"It was awful, Theron. And I know this is different. I know and yet..." I can't finish my sentence, fighting off the burn of tears in my eyes.

He leans in, rests his forehead against mine.

"If anything goes wrong, anything at all, I'll be on the first flight back or I'll steal a damn truck and drive through the night if I have to. You say the word, and I'll come home. You know that." He kisses my cheek, a quiet plea for understanding.

"I do." I whisper it before I can overthink it. "You came back last time. And you'll come back this time."

"I'm your Alpha," he says. "That means I show up. No matter what."

And for now, that will have to be enough.

"Then go," I whisper, burying myself in his chest, arms straining to pull him close despite the belly between us. "But make it quick."

CHAPTER 21
THERON

Last night was a bit of a mess.

With Rourke's last-minute call for work and trying to keep my Rosie from crying over me leaving, our typical night of kisses and cuddles turned into me desperately fucking all my frustrations out and into her.

I wasn't gentle or sweet. I was insatiable and rough.

There are dozens of little purple blotches scattered over her hips and thighs from my hands gripping her so damn tightly.

And yet, here she is curled into my chest, soft little breaths ghosting over my skin, her body loose and warm and so fucking perfect in the dim morning light and she sleeps soundly.

And I'm still inside her.

My knot, fat and swollen, is cradled by her sweet little cunt like it belongs there. Like it's never coming out. And God, the way she feels around me, wet and pulsing, like her body hasn't stopped aching for me even in sleep.

I groan quietly into her hair, tightening my grip around her waist. The scent of her arousal is still thick in the air. Not as wild as last night. No, this is softer. Honeyed. Dreamy. But it's still potent enough to make my cock twitch inside her.

She shifts in her sleep, her hips wiggle the slightest inch, and her pussy clenches around me like a vice.

Fuck.

I press my forehead to her shoulder, breathing her in.

Every inch of her smells like *mine*. My scent layered over hers, soaked into the bed.

And I can't help it.

My hips move, slow and instinctive, grinding forward just enough to make her walls flutter again. I bite back another groan as her body grips me tighter in response.

God, this Omega. She ruins me. Turns me into a single-minded idiot led only by her whims and my cock.

A sleepy whimper slips from her lips, barely more than a breath. My cock twitches again, and my knot pulses.

She's still needy. Still aching.

And I'm still not done with her.

My hand drifts over her stomach. I feel the stretch of her skin. The way her body makes room for the little life held within.

I hate that I have to leave. I hate that I'll miss even a day without her.

"I should let you sleep," I mumble against her skin, kissing her shoulder. Not sure if she is even awake enough to understand me. "But fuck, baby…you're still so tight around me. I need you."

She makes a soft noise, nuzzling back into me, and I feel her hips roll.

I guess she heard me.

I roll us gently, pressing her forward, to lay more on her side, careful not to dislodge my knot just yet. I grab her thigh, moving her leg to spread her open, her body pliant with the haze of sleep.

I start to move, lazy and deep, knot grinding in tight circles, stretching her pussy. She gasps awake with a soft cry, eyes fluttering as she reaches behind for me, gripping my hair.

"Alpha…" she breathes, voice raw and sweet.

"I'm here," I rasp, leaning forward to kiss her sloppily on the cheek. "Still inside you. Still hard for you, baby."

She blinks, dazed and already breathless as my cock starts to move again, slow thrusts that drag my swollen girth against her tender walls.

Her hand grips my hair, eyes glassy. "Theron…"

"I couldn't help it," I whisper, mouth brushing against her ear. "Woke up to your sweet little pussy clenching around me and my hand on your pregnant tummy."

She moans softly, her hips wiggling back to meet mine.

And it starts again. The slow build. The morning ache. The need that never really left.

Because soon, distance will stretch between us. And the thought of spending nights apart only adds teeth to the ache for touch, for closeness, for slow, sweet lovemaking like this.

Her body was made to answer every depraved hunger inside me. And mine was shaped to hold her gently, to worship every tender, beautiful part of her.

And this bed. Our bed. Was built for mornings like this. For warm tangled sheets. For whispered desire. For loving her like I never have to let go.

Because without her, I would be buried in her absence.

Her soft moan vibrates against my chest as her hips swing back, offering herself to me with breathless need.

There isn't a frantic pleading or desperate pleas here. Just perfect quiet wanting.

I pull back just enough to look at her.

Hair tangled across her pillow. Cheeks flushed. Lips pink and parted, still kiss-bruised from the night before. Her body shines with the lightest sheen of sweat.

God, she's so fucking pretty like this.

Sleep-warm, pregnant and cock-drunk, all while being stretched wide around my knot.

My hands slide down her hips, thumb brushing the softness of her stomach as I move in gentle rocking motions. This isn't a rough fucking, it's a moment of pure God-forsaken love making.

She gasps softly, arching against me.

"That's it," I murmur, lowering my mouth to her neck, kissing a path along her jaw, down to our bond mark. "Just like that, baby. Let me love you slow."

She shivers as my cock drags inside her, tugging against the stretch of her pussy. Her cunt clenches instinctively, pulsing with every movement, every sweet grind that presses my body deeper into hers.

Her fingers tangle in my hair as I nuzzle between her neck and shoulder, kissing her like she's something sacred. And she is.

"Theron," she sighs. "You feel so good…"

I groan against her skin, her hips rolling to the same tempo as mine, matching my rhythm, the slow roll of her body melting against me.

My hands tighten on her hips, guiding her.

"That's it, Rosie," I murmur, mouth trailing against her shoulder. "Ride it out with me, sweetheart. Nice and slow."

Her moans fill the space between us, sweet and lilting, like music created only for the depraved. Her cunt squeezes me with each slow thrust, her body welcoming me like a trap.

I slip one hand between her thighs, fingers finding her clit, already puffy and eager. She gasps, then sighs, hips stuttering when I rub gentle, lazy circles over that needy little bundle of nerves.

"Oh," she breathes, eyes fluttering. "I'm close… Theron!"

"I know," I murmur, pressing my forehead to hers.

I keep fucking her slow. Deep. Devoted. My mouth on her skin, my fingers teasing her clit, my cock dragging through her. Her body trembles, then tightens, sucking me in with greedy little pulses that make it harder and harder to hold back.

With a wail, her body melts into mine, cunt clenching hard around my cock, milking me with soft, rolling contractions that won't stop.

I groan, head falling back, hips grinding deeper, until I feel the telltale swell begin again. My knot. Thickening. Stretching.

And she takes it.

All of it.

Another gasp, another twitch of her hips as it locks firmly in place once more. And God, it's *heaven.*

I keep moving, just a quiet rocking of my hips. Burying my cock as deep as I can, while my fingers stay pressed to her swollen clit, coaxing another soft, whimpering release from her shaking body.

We move together in that blissful haze, love and lust tangled in soft morning light, until I feel that impossible tension winding tight in my spine.

I groan into her chest, every muscle straining.

With a low, guttural sound, I spill inside her, warmth flooding deep, pulsing past my knot until she's soaked and stretched and filled all over again.

And I kiss her.

Again. And again.

Her breathing softens, little by little, the tension in her body morphing into soft, sleepy weight against the mattress.

Still wrapped around me. Still tied.

My knot pulses one last time, but the urgency is gone now. Just a dull throb. A quiet, bittersweet kind of bliss that settles low with content.

She hums in her throat, barely a sound, as I stroke her hair with slow, steady fingers.

"You okay?" I murmur, brushing a kiss to her temple.

She nods, lips forming a faint smile. "Mmhmm…"

Her voice is thick with sleep, sweet and slurred.

"Good girl," I whisper, smiling against her skin. "You're perfect. You know that?"

She lets out a breath, soft, like a sigh, and I swear, even with her eyelids fluttering closed, she's still glowing. Still golden and warm and mine.

I kiss her, just a brush of lips, full of everything I can't fit into words.

"I love you, Rosie," I whisper against her mouth. "More than anything."

She doesn't answer. Her body relaxing as sleep tugs her back under its blanket.

And I hold her close, locked together again, still tangled in the sheets and whisper it again like a prayer to a God I don't even believe in.

"I love you."

Always.

CHAPTER 22
THERON

The sun isn't even high yet, but sweat clings to the back of my neck as I toss the last duffel into the truck bed. I should already be on the road. But I told Rourke I wasn't leaving before noon. The old bastard grumbled, of course, saying something about weather issues and logistics, but I didn't care. I'm not missing this tour. Not when this house feels so right for us.

I slam the tailgate closed and glance back at the house, our house, for now. It's small, safe and crowded in a way that makes Rosie curl up closer to me at night.

She doesn't complain. But I see her mind going a million miles a minute, worrying about the space we don't have.

I saw the way her fingers paused on every page of that baby catalog like she was mentally measuring each spare inch we have. The way she touches the walls of the nursery-turned-library-turned-back with a look that says *that won't work, and neither will that.*

This new place though? I can picture it already.

The den off the hallway, small and sunlit. I'll build her shelves from scratch for her books. A little ladder that can glide on a secure rail. Cozy seating. Her stuffed animals everywhere. A space just for her, without faded dreams to haunt her.

And that back bedroom? The one facing east?

Pale yellow walls. A soft rug. A cradle I'll sand and stain myself. Maybe a mural with stars or flowers or a sleeping bear, whatever my Rosie wants.

God, I want to give her all of it.

I want to give our baby all of it.

The front door creaks open, and whatever breath I had left in my chest gets stolen clean out of me.

Rosie steps outside in a soft yellow dress that hugs every curve of her pregnant belly. The color makes her glow, like sunshine with hips. Her hair's loose around her shoulders, skin glowing, and her hand instinctively rests just beneath the swell of her stomach as she locks the door behind her.

I'm pretty sure my heart stops. And my dick wakes up, ready for another round this fine morning.

"Sweetheart," I call, crossing the driveway to meet her. "You know it's illegal to walk around looking that edible in broad daylight, right?"

She snorts, but the faint blush in her cheeks tells me she doesn't mind being devoured by my eyes.

"Stop ogling me and open the damn door," she mutters, half-smiling.

"Yes ma'am."

I open the truck door and help her with both hands, one braced on her lower back, the other guiding under her thigh like she might break if I don't hold her just right. She rolls her eyes but lets me do it anyway, grumbling something about how I treat her like a porcelain doll instead of a hormonal ogre with swollen ankles.

Once she's settled, seatbelt buckled and dress smoothed, I close her door gently and jog around to the driver's side, climbing in with a huff.

She eyes me sideways as I start the engine.

"This is ridiculous, you know."

"What is?"

"This." She gestures lazily toward the road. "Driving to the house tour, then driving back here, then you driving to the airport. It's like a triangle of wasted fuel. I could've just driven myself."

"Nope." I glance at her, grin tugging at the corner of my mouth. "Not happening. You and that baby you're carrying are the only reason I breathe."

My smile falters, and my tone goes stiff. "I'm not letting you drive to the end of the damn block without me right now."

"Okay. No driving." Her smile is soft, but I catch the way she turns her face to the window, probably a little irritated with me.

I reach for her hand across the console, linking our fingers together.

"Besides," I murmur, bringing her knuckles to my lips, "I like the idea of doing this together. One last calm before I disappear into the mountains for a few days."

She squeezes back. "Then let's make it count."

The rest of our thirty-minute drive is quiet, except for my truly awful rendition of "When You Say Nothing at All" by Keith Whitley. I sing with my full chest and zero pitch, one hand tapping the steering wheel while the other holds Rosie's.

She laughs her butt off as she tries to sing along with me, but my terrible performance gives her the giggles, stealing her breath in a way that I don't think was intended with this song.

The gravel crunches under the tires as we pull into the long driveway, tree branches bowing overhead like a quiet welcome. The house sits nestled in the middle of the lot, all soft edges and weathered charm. White shutters a little crooked andsiding faded by sun and time. It's not perfect. But it's close.

Cottage-style, just like Rosie likes. Built in the 60s with a stone chimney and low-pitched roof, plus a second wing that juts off the left like an afterthought, clearly part of the 2000s addition the listing mentioned. The place has good bones. A little bruised, sure, but nothing I can't fix. Hell, with the right touch, I can make it shine.

"Alright," I murmur, parking. "Let's see if this one's really it."

Rosie's quiet, eyes flicking over the front porch, the wildflowers blooming in tangles near the walkway. I can see her imagining it already.

I round the truck, open her door, and help her down slowly—hand braced on the back of her thigh as she lands. She gives me a look like I'm being silly.

Just as I close the door, a voice calls from the side path.

"Hi there! You must be the Blackwoods!"

A short, curvy woman approaches with a clipboard in one hand and a bouncy wave in the other. Her dress is floral and bright, her hair pinned up in a messy bun that still somehow looks intentional. Her energy is sunshine and rainbows, and it's just what we need.

"That's us," I say, nodding as Rosie steps beside me.

"I'm Daisy," the woman beams. "Your realtor. Sorry I'm a few minutes late. I was wrangling a cat out of the utility shed."

Rosie smiles. "I'm Rosie."

The two women blink at each other for a moment, then grin at the exact same time, like sharing a secret joke that I'm obviously missing.

"Rosie and Daisy," Rosie laughs, shaking her head. "Sounds like a garden party."

"I was *just* thinking that!" Daisy giggles. "I don't get to meet many floral namesakes, so this is already my favorite showing today."

They share a warm chuckle, and I swear, just like that, Rosie's shoulders drop a little. Good. She needs to feel safe here and be able to picture herself here.

Daisy waves us toward the porch.

"So! Like the listing said, this home was built in 1962. The addition on the left was done in '04. It added the fourth bedroom, a second living space, and upgraded the master suite."

Inside, the scent of dust and potential hits me first. The foyer opens into a broad hallway with uneven tile that creaks under my boots. The kitchen is off to the right and it's huge. The footprint is fantastic. Center island, tons of light, enough room for a breakfast nook and whatever else my Rosie might want.

But the tile is cracked and hideous. The cabinets are still painted that weird off-white every house from 1998 seemed to love. And the carpet running into the dining area is a sin against good taste.

"Needs hardwood," I mutter.

Rosie trails a hand over the island countertop. "And maybe pale green cabinets."

I smile at her comment. "Pale green cabinets and maybe we can DIY some resin white counter tops to keep the renovation budget down."

"That is a brilliant idea.," Daisy says, nodding. "If you plan for updates yourselves, you might have room to negotiate a lower offer. Sellers are more flexible when buyers aren't demanding costly repairs upfront." With that, she turns and leads us deeper into the house.

The tour winds through the den. It's a little small, but flooded with morning light. Perfect for her books.

I'm already building the shelves in my head. Knotted oak, wide and deep, maybe a space she can nap beneath.

We move down the hallway finding the four bedrooms, just like we were promised. The first two are plain, easy to work with. The third, tucked in the back, faces east.

"This one gets the sunrise," Daisy notes.

Rosie steps in, quiet, soaking it in. I can practically see it: yellow walls, a crib, soft rugs and plush toys. The beginning of everything.

We save the master suite for last and it's worth it.

The walk-in closet is massive. The ensuite bathroom has an oversized tub, dual sinks, and a window that looks out into the trees.

"This is it," I say quietly, speaking more for Rosie than Daisy.

She doesn't answer. A solemn look of concern on her face.

She just takes my hand.

"I should give you two a moment." Daisy says with a polite tone. "I'll be outside if you have any questions."

She turns, walking out the door, leaving us alone to speak amongst ourselves.

Rosie exhales, eyes drifting slowly around the master suite. She hesitates to speak, standing beside me, trying to gather all her thoughts.

"Can we sit for a second?"

I nod and lead her to the edge of a bed frame left behind by the owner. It's just a metal rail right now, no mattress, but it'll do for a quick sit.

She lowers herself with a soft grunt, one hand on her belly. I stay standing, too keyed up to sit.

"This house needs work," she says quietly. "The tile's shot. The carpet has to go. The kitchen will need gutting. And we can't afford any of this unless we sell the house we're in now."

I crouch in front of her, one hand braced on her thigh. "I know."

"It's not perfect. No nursery yet. That den's small. And we'll need time."

"I know."

"It's going to take time and money, and we don't even have a proper timeline or—"

"Sweetheart." I reach up, gently taking her face in my hands.

"This is where our kids are going to grow up. Right here. I can feel it."

Her eyes fall closed, and her head hangs low. "You say 'kids'...but we aren't even sure if that can happen."

I blink, caught off guard. "Is one not enough?"

The question baffles me. My brows furrow. "What do you mean?"

She exhales, lifting her head and her eyes, glassy and unsure, stare into mine. "First, it was *if* we could get pregnant. Then it was finding a new, big house. Now you're talking about more kids. And I..." She falters but finds her words quickly continuing. "I'm terrified I won't be able to give you all the things you keep dreaming of."

The hurt in her voice is corrosive, burning its way through my chest. God, she really thinks that's what this is about.

I laugh softly, not at her, but at how wrong she's gotten it. I reach up, brushing my hand gently through her hair, then rest my palm atop her head like I can soothe away all those silly worries she's got floating around in her head.

"Rosie, baby," cupping her face with both hands now so she can't look away, "my love for you has never been, and never will be, measured by what you can give me."

Her eyes search for some sign of a lie, but she won't find any.

"I would love you if it was just us. No baby. No big house. No nursery full of tiny shoes and over-priced toys." My thumbs brush across her cheeks. "But if we're blessed with more?" I shrug. "That's a miracle. But not a requirement."

"But I know you, Rosie. I know what you dream about. A cozy home. Laughter in every room. A little chaos and a lot of love. A house full of kids tumbling through the hallways and muddy shoes by the door. And if that's still your dream, then yeah, I'm going to try like hell to give it to you. For you."

Her eyes soften, and the breath she lets out is less worried, more awed. Her gaze sweeps the bathroom, the closet, the windows framing the trees like a painting.

"This is it," she whispers, attention returning to me. "This is our home."

Something breaks loose in my chest—hot, wild, and undeniable.

I jump up from my crouching position and sweep her into my arms like I've waited years to do it, spinning her in one tight circle as her laughter bursts out, sweet and bright and all fucking mine. She clutches my shoulders, dress billowing, belly between us like a living promise.

I kiss her. Hard and hungry and maybe just a hint of feral. Like I need to taste her joy to believe it's real. Like I want to devour the moment and burn it into my blood.

She gasps into my mouth, her body going soft in my arms, pliant and trusting. I grip her tighter.

The beautiful image of kids screaming and laughing in the yard. Mud on their knees, grass in their hair. Rosie barefoot on the porch with another baby on the way, round and glowing and yelling at them to come wash up before dinner.

My mate, full of life, full of love, and full of *me*.

The image slams into me so hard it makes my dick throb.

I pull back just enough to whisper against her lips, voice wrecked with emotion and need.

"I'm going to build this life for us, Rosie. I swear it. You and me, and whatever kind of beautiful chaos life blesses us with."

"This is already more than enough," she whispers against my cheek. "You've made my dreams come true, my Alpha."

I would tear this world apart and rebuild it just for her. And God help anything that tries to take this dream from us.

CHAPTER 23
ROSIE

I take another slow sip of water, ignoring how much I already have to pee, and eye the half-empty bottle like it personally offends me.

Thirty-four weeks.

That's how far along I am today. Which means Theron's been gone for nearly three months.

What was supposed to be a four-day job has stretched into eighty-four days of nonstop site-hopping. And now? If the weather doesn't clear or someone else doesn't get their ass up the mountain, I'm staring down the barrel of week thirteen without him.

I shift on the couch, propping my swollen feet higher on the cushions. The baby gives a lazy roll, more a stretch sensation than a kick and I rub a hand over the tight curve of my belly, sighing.

"Yeah," I mumble. "I miss him too."

The house is quiet. Too quiet. No boots by the door. No grumbling

Alpha from the kitchen because I "forgot" to drink enough water.

I glance at the side table. Three empty water bottles sit like trophies.

"Look, Alpha. I'm being good." I grin to myself with thoughts of his praise. But then I just feel silly saying that out loud.

Yesterday, during our video call, he gave me the full lecture. Hydration. Rest. Avoid stress. Don't lift anything heavier than a feather. I rolled my eyes through half of it, but the truth is… I cling to it. His voice. His concern. His presence, even if it was just through a screen.

I haven't seen him in person since I was twenty-three weeks. Now I'm thirty-four, almost thirty-five.

And the baby bump he kissed goodbye has turned into a full, round belly that makes getting off the couch an Olympic sport. I rub my hand across it, grateful. So, so grateful. But God, I wish he was here to see it.

As if summoned by the thought, my phone buzzes on the armrest.

I snatch it up, answering so fast I nearly drop it.

"Hi," I breathe.

"Hey, sweetheart." His voice is low, crackling through the weak signal.

"Are you packed?" I ask, too eager. "Did they clear the road?"

He's quiet for half a second too long and my heart drops.

"Rosie…" he sighs. "I'm not getting out tomorrow."

"What?"

"One of the supply trucks got stranded. Rourke's pulling me in to lead the second team." The static of the weak phone signal is loud, almost drowning him out.

"It's just one more week."

One more week.

That's what he said last time.

And the time before that.

"Okay," I say softly. Because what else can I say?

He hears it in my voice. Of course he does.

"I hate this," he says. "I hate being away. But I swear, Rosie. I'm coming home soon. I'm counting the days."

I nod, even though he can't see it.

"I know," I whisper. "Just hurry, okay? I'm going to be in labor before you can get here."

"Don't say that, baby," he murmurs. "I've already missed too much. Don't make me imagine missing more." The static grows louder, finally drowning him out completely.

"Theron? I can't hear you." I try to raise my voice over the sound of the weak signal but it's fruitless.

The line cuts. Just a soft click and silence, followed by that gutting little *beep-beep-beep* that confirms what I already know.

The silence that follows feels cruel. Like a door slamming shut on a breath I wasn't finished taking.

I stare at the screen for a few seconds before setting the phone face down on my belly and exhaling slowly.

"One more week."

I whisper it again. And though I am disappointed I'm more angry at that jerk of a boss of his. Then next time I see that asshole Rourke, I'm going to give him a damn piece of my mind.

Doesn't he know I'm pregnant? Probably, if I know Theron, he's told the man every time he speaks to him.

At least Daisy's been keeping me busy.

We put in an offer on the house the same day we toured it; we didn't want to risk the chance of it slipping through our hands if we waited. And to our utter shock, it was accepted within the week.

That part felt easy. Like fate. Like the universe whispering *yes, this is yours.*

But now?

We have to sell this place.

And God, it's taking a hell of a lot more effort than either of us expected.

Daisy's been a saint, fielding lowball offers, scheduling back-to-back showings, even helping me stage the library to look more like a guest room with borrowed linens and fake succulents from her cousin's shop downtown. But it's not enough. Not yet.

Every potential buyer walks in and all they see is *small.*

Too small for a growing family. Too cramped. Too dated. Too close to the road. Too full of our memories, maybe.

But I'm hopeful. I know it'll happen. Eventually.

But between swollen feet, long nights, and Theron's absence stretching longer with each call, "eventually" feels like a cruel kind of hope.

I press a hand to my belly again, feeling the baby shift beneath my palm.

"You're going to love the new house," I whisper. "Bookshelves and big windows and a backyard just waiting for you."

Another week.

I close my eyes and try to believe it.

The phone rings again.

I snatch it up, half hopping it's Theron somehow reconnecting but sadly it's not. It's Daisy.

"Hey, Rosie!" Her voice is bright, but a little rushed. "Sorry to bother you, but I've got a full schedule today and I need those bank statements for the lender package. Do you remember? You were going to email them two days ago?"

Shit.

I close my eyes and sigh. "Damn it… I totally forgot. Pregnancy brain is real, I swear."

Daisy chuckles on the other end, not unkind. "I figured. Listen, no pressure, but if I don't get those today, we're looking at a delay on final approval. Any chance you can swing by? I'll be in my office for the next few hours."

I glance down at my belly, at the spot where baby just rolled again like they're gently nudging me forward. I've barely left the house this week. I've just been too tired, and too swollen to even think of leaving. But this? This is important.

"Yeah," I say, already shifting to sit up and groaning at the effort. "I'll be there in…an hour? Does that work for you?"

"Perfect," Daisy chirps. "I'll print the forms you need. See you soon."

I smile despite myself. "Thanks, Daisy."

We hang up, and I let the phone fall to the couch cushion beside me. Alright.

Get dressed. Get your purse. And get this done.

Just a short drive. A simple errand to get us one step closer to our dream home. And staying busy means time passes quicker.

It's harmless.

And what Theron doesn't know won't kill him… I hope.

CHAPTER 24
ROURKE

My phone's lit up with alerts from three sites, there's four emails left unread in my inbox on my open computer, and a logistics spreadsheet that looks like it was filled out by a drunk intern on my desk. All while the rain outside my office window drums steady against the glass.

"Christ," I mutter, dragging a hand down my face. The last three damn months have been nothing but duct-taped chaos. Delayed supply drops. Two broken-down transports. A Beta foreman who decided now was the perfect time to quit while on the top of fucking Mount Helen. And what do I do?

I call Theron.

Again.

And again.

Because he's the only bastard I trust to clean up a mess without crying about it.

I've known Theron since he was twenty. A wild rebellious brat who thought the world owed him something. But he had the kind of grit you don't teach. The kind that doesn't blink in a firefight or flinch when everything goes sideways. I built half this company with him at my six. Hell, I might trust him more than I trust myself.

And now I've got him traveling from job to job, with impossible distances from the woman who'd bleed for him. All because no one else can keep their shit together. Myself included, apparently.

But even he's starting to become a problem. I've already had three calls about a growling Alpha with a fuse down to the wick.

The man is becoming feral with absence. And I can't blame him.

His mate is pregnant and what started as a quick four-day job has turned into a marathon of bullshit. He should've been home a week ago. Hell, way more than that, but the hits just keep coming. And I keep sending him out, because no one else can fix it.

I lit him up for bailing on his last job. Told him a job didn't run on sentiment. That he'd damn near lost us a contract going rogue during his mate's heat. And now here I am. Piling shit on his back and pretending like it's just another week at the office. Like he doesn't have a woman counting the minutes and a kid kicking inside her while he's covering my ass out in the field. I'm a Goddamn hypocrite.

I rub at the back of my neck, feeling the weight of it all. It's not just the jobs, but what it's costing him. What I'm asking of him.

My phone rings again.

"Son of a bitch," I growl, snatching it off the desk and checking the number. Unknown, but it's a local line.

Probably that supplier I can never get ahold of finally delivered the med packs we've been waiting for. Or it could be the warehouse calling to say we finally ran out of them.

I answer with a bite in my voice. "Rourke. Make it quick."

"Hello, this Sarah, from Oakland Hospital. I'm calling in hopes of reaching Mr. Theron Blackwood. He's listed as the primary emergency contact for a patient currently in our care, and we've been trying to reach him urgently with little success."

The anger in my blood runs cold and my face drains of color. My body goes still.

"It's important he comes in as soon as possible."

"Why? What happened?"

"I'm sorry sir but I can't disclose private information. Please make sure he gets here as soon as possible. It's extremely urgent. Thank you."

The line goes dead. I stare at the phone for a moment, the dial tone echoing like a threat in my ear.

A rush of anger surges through me and I slam my fist into the desk so hard the monitor rattles.

"Fuck!"

I think of her face. Rose. I've seen her a handful of times over the years. I remember when she dropped off something for him at HQ. I thought she was ridiculous, smiling like a kid at a candy store just for a two-second conversation with her mate.

But Theron would've razed cities to keep that look safe. And I sent him to the middle of fucking nowhere.

My chair scrapes against the floor as I shoot up. I grab my keys from the hook by the door, heart already pounding, boots hammering against the tile as I charge out of the office and down the hall. Heads turn.

Someone opens their mouth to speak but I don't stop.

Rose is in the hospital and Theron isn't here because I'm the son of a bitch who kept him away.

If he throws a punch at me, it'll be because I fucking deserve it. I actually hope he does hit me. Maybe it'll put my damn priorities straight.

The rain strikes like bullets the second I shove out the front door, but I don't flinch, running toward my Bronco and throwing myself into the driver's seat, fumbling with my key before turning the ignition and peeling out of the lot like the devil's on my tail.

She's not my mate. Hell, there isn't even a drop of blood between us, but I've watched that Alpha bleed for them across state lines, and I owe him more than a voicemail.

Traffic out of downtown is a nightmare, but I don't have time to bitch about it, but damn this is going to add another ten minutes before I can get to the hospital.

One hand is gripping the wheel hard enough to leave marks, while my other hand digs into the console, pulling out a satellite phone. It's clunky and outdated but it's the only way I'm going to reach him with him being so far out in the wilds.

My thumb hovers for half a second over the call button.

Beta Gem Falls is three hours out of town. Maybe more with the rain. And if he hits a patch of washed-out road, he's going to lose his shit.

I hit *dial*.

One ring.

Two.

"Come on, Blackwood!" I shout at the phone. This idiot needs to answer dammit.

My hand's slick on the wheel. Not from the rain but sweat and nausea. From the cold weight in my gut that hasn't let up since that woman from the hospital called.

A third ring and finally he answers.

"Rourke?"

CHAPTER 25
THERON

"Rourke?"

Static crackles through the line. I press the sat phone tighter to my ear and squint out the windshield. Rain slices across the glass, thick and gray like a damn cliché. The weather acting as moody as me.

There's more static. Muffled words. Something that sounds like my name but twisted through a gravel filter.

"If you're calling me for another damn job," I growl, shifting in the driver's seat, "you're out of your Goddamn mind."

I'm less than four hours from home. From Rosie. From her belly that's grown rounder and more beautiful since I saw her last.

This was supposed to be the last run. Do a supply drop for the detail in Beta Gem falls and take lead for the week and then get the fuck out when someone else was finally available. I've given him every spare ounce of loyalty I've got left in me. And now I'm wrung out. I'm fucking done.

"Theron—listen—"

Rourke's voice finally cuts through, garbled but urgent.

"What?" I snap. "You're breaking up."

"No—it's Rosie—"

Rain pounds the truck and my heart sinks into an abyss I'm terrified to look into.

The static buzzes on the phone. "What about Rosie?" I bark, already reaching for the GPS, already shifting gears but the silence after I ask feels like someone is about to stab me through the heart.

Every part of me clenches, waiting for a word that won't shatter me. My pulse is a war drum in my ears. My mouth tastes like ash.

When Rourke finally speaks, the blade sinks into my chest.

"…hospital called" his voice crackles, rough and rushed. "She's— Oakland hospital."

My heart stumbles. Static whines through the line, swallowing pieces of the message like a cruel joke.

My grip tightens around the phone, "What happened?"

"Couldn't—Urgent—" The words warp, cut short by bad reception.

My skin prickles with goosebumps. My vision tunnels.

"Rourke? What happened!?" I demand but the line goes dead.

My stomach lurches. The cab of the truck feels like it's closing in on me and every muscle locks like I'm stuck in a nightmare.

But I can't wake up from this. Because it's real.

I floor the gas.

The tires scream as I round the curve, mud spitting up against the wheel wells. The rain's coming harder now, slapping the windshield like it's trying to keep me from her. Wipers can't keep up. But it's fine, I know this road. I'll make it. I'll make sure I do.

I have to stay focused. I have to keep my head on straight. I can't spiral. I can't give in to the *what ifs*.

She could be fine. Just a dizzy spell. Maybe Braxton Hicks. That's normal at this stage, right?

She's thirty-four weeks pregnant.

Thirty-four.

I slam my fist into the steering wheel, the sharp crack echoing in the cabin. A cold rush floods my veins. A poisonous mix of fear and fury I can't shake.

And just like that, the spiral I was fighting crashes through me anyway.

What if something's wrong with the baby?

What if she fell?

What if she passed out?

What if she's in a hospital bed, gasping for air with no one holding her hand?

What if she called for me, and I didn't answer?

I told her I'd show up.

What if I lose them both, and all because I picked the job one more fucking time?

My grip tightens on the steering wheel until the bones in my hands ache. The truck veers hard into the next lane and I jerk it back.

I can't drive fast enough. Every truck or slow car feels like a punishment or a personal enemy. My hands are white-knuckled on the wheel, heart hammering so loud I can't hear the engine anymore. All I can think about is her.

Rosie. My mate. My everything. I need to see her. Just one look, one squeeze of her hand to prove she's okay.

I keep thinking of her belly. How much it's grown since I've left. How big our baby has grown inside her.

How I rested my hand there at night and whispered stories, telling them tales they'd never come to know. All just to hear Rosie laugh and say, *"They already know your voice."*

I keep replaying the last time I touched her, really touched her. The way she leaned into me when I kissed her temple. The soft sound she made when I whispered that I'd be back soon. Her stomach pressed to mine like a heartbeat I could hold.

The phone buzzes again on the seat beside me. Probably Rourke. Maybe the hospital. Maybe the world crashing down in one more notification.

I ignore it. Eyes locked forward.

Just let me get there.

Let her be okay.

Let our baby be okay.

I don't care what I have to do. What I have to give.

God, don't take them from me.

CHAPTER 26
ROSIE

Pain blooms fast. White-hot and everywhere.

My side burns. My head pounds. Something sticky drips down my temple.

A car alarm screams nearby—sharp and relentless—and I don't know where I am. The sky above me spins. Glass glitters like ice in the corner of my vision.

I try to move. But I can't, like I'm being restrained.

Everything feels stiff. Heavy. My fingers twitch once before they go still again. Something tightens around my middle, deep and cramping and *wrong*

Oh God. No.

The baby.

No.

No no no no no—

I try to call out, but my throat's too dry. My lips part, and all I can manage is one word.

"…Theron."

CHAPTER 27
THERON

The hospital lobby doors fly open with a hiss of air and the slap of wet boots on linoleum. I charge through them like a man possessed.

"Rose Blackwood," I bark, already moving toward the front desk. "Where is she?"

The woman behind the counter startles, eyes wide as she scrambles to pull up the system.

"I—uh—one moment—"

"Rose Blackwood!" I shout again, voice rising, chest heaving. "*Where is she?!*"

The people in the waiting room go silent. A chair creaks. My hands slam against the counter hard enough to rattle the plastic donation bin.

The poor receptionist fumbles the keyboard, trying to speak through her panic. "Sir, I'm pulling up the—"

"Where is she?!" The words tear from my throat. Fury. Fear. Love.

All of it boiling over. I can't breathe with her name in limbo.

Two security guards move toward me from the far side of the room, palms lifted like they're about to talk down a bomb.

"Sir," one of them says carefully. "Calm down. Let us help you—"

"I'm looking for my *mate!*" I snarl, stepping back from the desk, turning toward them. "*Rose Blackwood!* Thirty-four weeks pregnant. *I need to know what happened!*"

I hang my head. "Please…"

I'm desperate. I need to find her. To see her. To know that this nightmare isn't my reality.

"Blackwood!"

The voice cracks through the noise.

I spin just in time to see Rourke pushing through a set of elevator doors, his expression dark and urgent.

"She's in the emergency room," he says fast, already motioning for me to follow. "They're trying to stabilize her."

My stomach drops through the floor. I take off without another word, boots echoing against the tile as I chase him toward the elevators. Every step is a scream in my chest.

What happened to her?

What happened to our baby?

Please, God, *don't let me be too late.*

Rourke doesn't look back. Just storms through the halls like a man on a mission, and I follow, dodging nurses, carts, and the stale stink of antiseptic and burnt coffee.

He pushes through the double doors into the ER wing, and the chaos hits like a wall.

Voices everywhere. Machines beeping. A woman crying behind a curtain. Someone screaming down the hall.

I catch a glimpse of an inmate chained to a bed, a guard standing just behind him. The guy grins at me as we pass.

I shove down the animalistic snarl rising in my throat.

Rourke slows for just a second. "Theron…"

The tone makes me pause.

He's bracing me.

"What happened?" I grind out, barely managing to keep my voice level. "Tell me."

He exhales, jaw tight. "She was driving. On her way to meet the realtor."

My heart lurches.

"Some kid was coming down the hill," he continues, quieter now. "His brakes went out. Lost control."

The words land like concrete. Heavy. Impossible to hold.

"He tried to stop. Witnesses said he did everything he could. It was an accident."

No. No, this can't be just an accident. I need someone to blame. I need someone to hate. Something. Anything to point my anger at so it makes sense. Because if this is just some cruel twist of fate, some meaningless act of God, then how the hell am I supposed to cope? How do I claw my way through this if there's no one to scream at, no throat to rip open, no punishment to deal out?

The kid? Some teen who probably panicked behind the wheel and couldn't control the car? What do I do with that? He's probably scared shitless, maybe hurt himself. Do I go after him, just so I have someone to bleed?

Rosie? Never. Even if she knew I didn't want her driving. Even if I told her over and over again that she needed to rest, that I'd handle everything.

But she's stubborn, and brave, and always trying to go the extra mile just for me. She probably thought she was doing the right thing. She thought it was a small errand. Something quick and harmless.

Daisy, then. The realtor Rourke mentioned. If she asked Rosie to come out today. Maybe she pushed when she shouldn't have, maybe that's where the fault lies. But even as the thought forms, it collapses. There's no proof. No target.

There's no one to blame.

And that is what makes this unbearable. Because if this is no one's fault, then it's everyone's loss. And it makes me want to scream until my throat tears open. I can't fight an accident. I can't kill bad luck. And I don't know how to survive something I can't destroy.

We round the corner, and the glowing red letters of **Trauma 2** greets us with its ugly appearance as they hang above the doors where I fear my Rosie will be.

But those doors burst open. A swarm of nurses flood the hallway, clustered around a gurney. They're shouting numbers. Vitals, O2 levels, stats I can't even begin to understand. Their voices blur together, speaking too fast and shouting over the noise of the emergency room.

And on that gurney is my Rosie.

She's unconscious and pale. An IV runs from her arm, an oxygen mask covers her face. There are bruises along her arms, dried blood on her temple but I don't see a source to it. A fetal monitor is strapped around her pregnant stomach, beeping in a steady, haunting rhythm.

I don't know what I'm hearing. But I pray to whatever deity hears me, that it's our baby's heart. Steady and strong and still holding on.

"Rosie…" I whisper, stepping toward her with slow careful steps, like if I make a single wrong move, she'll shatter right before my eyes and leave me in this messy world alone.

Everything fades around her. The hospital. The hallway. The storm of people beside her, all working to keep her heart beating, and our baby alive.

I reach for her. I just want to touch her. To feel the heat of her skin. To glide my hand over her heart and feel it beat. Anything to prove she's still here.

But a nurse steps into my path, arms outstretched. "Sir, you need to step back."

The words don't land. I barely hear them. "That's my mate," I mutter, dazed. "Rose Blackwood. She's mine."

I move forward again. Determination coursing through me, but another nurse grabs my arm. Then another. They try to push me back, corral me like I'm some loose, panicked animal.

And that's exactly what I've become.

I thrash and snarl. Ripping my arm free and reaching again. "Get out of my way!"

"Theron!" Rourke's voice yells above the rest, and his hands land on my shoulders wrenching me back, but even he's not going to stop me.

I push and push. "She needs me! Get the fuck off me! She needs me!" I shout, voice shaking as my chest heaves, eyes locked on her broken, unmoving body.

Chaos builds. Shouting and more arms try to hold me. My pulse thunders, ready to tear the entire hospital apart if I have to. Just to touch her. To feel her.

"Everyone step back." A commanding voice slices through the noise like a scalpel. The multitude of hands on me still, and so do I, surprisingly.

A doctor steps forward. "He's the mate," she says with cool authority. "Let him go."

The staff hesitates. Then parts, a sea of scrubs opens up and I stumble toward the gurney. Breath breaking, hands trembling. And finally, my fingers spread across her chest.

She's warm.

Her breaths are shallow, but they're there. Her heart still beats beneath my palm. It's faint, like a whisper trying to be heard in a chaotic storm.

"I'm here, Rosie," My voice is weak, the words catching against the sob rising in my throat. My hand trembles as I lift it to her cheek, brushing a streak of dried blood with aching tenderness. I'm here, baby… Please wake up. Please, just open your eyes."

My voice breaks.

I want her to laugh. To call me dramatic. To tell me I worry too much and that everything's fine. I want her to squeeze my hand and say she loves me. Just one more time.

But she doesn't stir. No matter how much I beg.

"Theron?"

A hand touches my shoulder. Gentle this time. Not trying to hold me back or pull me away. Just a soft touch, grounding and sorrowful.

"Theron, please listen to me."

I know this voice. I don't need to look to know it's Dr. Bryant. But I can't take my eyes off Rosie. Can't stop drinking her in like this might be the last time.

She's so still. So pale. My heart cracks open inside my chest.

"The impact of the crash caused a placental abruption."

The words slide past me at first, foreign and clinical, like she expects me to know what the hell that means. I shake my head, lips parting.

"Please… I don't understand."

My eyes stay on Rosie, but I strain to hear the explanation, because I have to understand.

"It means the placenta has detached from the uterus. The baby's oxygen supply is compromised…and both their lives are in danger."

No.

My stomach drops, cold and nauseous.

"We need to take her into surgery. An emergency delivery is the best chance to save them both."

"It's too early," I rasp, swinging my head toward Dr. Bryant. My voice breaks, my chest heaves. "It's too early."

"Yes," she says, calmly but firmly. "But it's our only option. And I need to be honest with you, Theron."

I turn back to Rosie, thumb brushing her cheekbone, memorizing the shape of her face, the way her lashes rest against her skin. She doesn't even know she's about to give birth.

Dr. Bryant continues.

"There might come a moment when I have to choose between them."

My heart stops.

"What?"

"I'm not saying it will happen," she rushes to clarify, "but if it does… if we're forced into that position…I need your consent. I need your decision. Rosie or the baby?"

"No." I shake my head violently. "No, you save them both. You save them both, dammit!"

"I will. If I can." Her voice softens. "But if it comes down to it, I need to know what she would want. What you want."

I look at Rosie again.

My mate.

My everything.

Our baby is a dream we've carried in our hearts, but she is the reason that dream exists at all.

I trace the edge of her lip with my thumb, fighting the scream in my chest. The pressure in my skull is unbearable. My eyes blur with tears.

I already know the answer, because it's carved into my very soul.

"I can't live without her."

My voice is hollow. Barely audible.

I swallow the pain, the fear, the guilt that I know will haunt me forever.

"Her."

CHAPTER 28
ROSIE

It begins in gold.

Warm and low and endless, like sunlight pressing through a curtain just before you wake. It's soft, not bright or shining like metal. It's the embodiment of warmth. The same warmth you feel in a lover's embrace.

I don't know where I am.

But I'm not afraid.

Yet suddenly the gold shifts. It's color changing, blooming into a soft pink form the corners of my vision. The shade is like the inside of a seashell. Like the blush of a first kiss. The memory comes with it, riding the color like a tide.

His hand in my hair.

The sound of rain.

The taste of him.

Our first kiss was shy and sure all at once. His breath hitched, and I remember thinking, *this is the one. The pair to my soul. My mate.*

The pink deepens, folds into red. Not harsh. Not bloody. Deep and full. The color of a kitchen light late at night. Of tomato soup and burning grilled cheese. Of bare feet and rumbling stomachs and him wrapping his arms around me from behind.

"Love you," I'd mumbled, between bites of gooey grilled cheese.

He'd kissed the crown of my head and whispered, "More than you'll know."

I laugh, even now, even here. Wherever that is.

Purple bleeds in slowly.

Deep and thick. The color of bruised dusk. Of velvet shadows. Of heat coiled low in my belly.

It wraps around me like a memory that doesn't ask permission. One that hums under the skin and drips with want.

His mouth on my neck.

His voice wrecked in my ear.

"You're mine, Rosie. Say it."

My skin had burned where his hands gripped my hips.

Where his teeth found that place on my shoulder. His mark.

Where his knot caught deep and kept me trembling and full.

That night he touched me like he was terrified I'd disappear.

That night I let him. We bonded forever that night. And it was perfect.

The color shifts again. Sky blue, like the color of my dreams. My hopes. The dream of a positive test. The one that came true.

I can still feel the weight of the pregnancy stick in my palm. Still see the lines forever ingrained in my memory. Those two magical lines that changed everything.

My hands had shaken. My knees had buckled.

"Thank you," he said.

As if I hadn't just turned both our lives inside out.

Blue melts into yellow. *Yellow*. His favorite color on me. That stupid sunshine dress that hugged the swell of my belly.

I see him looking at me across the kitchen, a grin fixed on his mouth, eyes dark with something reverent and unholy all at once. Plans shared to create a home perfect for us.

A nursery, painted in the same shade of yellow. A window where the morning light shines through every day.

I see the way he reached for me like I was gravity.

The baby had kicked that day, just once.

His eyes lit up like he'd never seen a miracle before.

The color shifts again. Darker now. Like dusk. Like the end.

Is this what it feels like? The end? When everything you love plays behind your eyes like a film reel made of light and want?

Heat flares in my chest, sharp and sudden. Like breath catching mid-sob.

I want to cry.

I am crying. Somewhere. Somehow.

I feel it all.

The scent of pine and leather and home surrounds me. Drowns me. Anchors me in a sea of color and memory and love so big it could tear me open from the inside out.

I want him.

I want tomorrow.

To wake in our too-small bed. To feel him kiss my hip before slipping out of the sheets. To hear the kettle whistle and pretend it annoys me.

To feel our baby roll beneath my palm and know, we made this.

I want pale green cabinets and chipped mugs and muddy footprints on the back porch.

I want lullabies sung off-key and tears wiped with kisses and books stacked on every surface because we never finished building the shelves.

I want to live it all.

Every imperfect, sacred second.

Because I love him.

Because this love has teeth and wings and roots.

Because I'm not done yet.

I want it. All of it. Every breath. Every shiver. Every laugh that made my fat belly shake.

Somewhere inside this color-soaked dream, this ache of memory and hope, something awakens.

A flutter beneath my ribs.

A ripple.

Still here.

Still fighting.

And somewhere, flickering at the edge of the dark…gold. Not light. Not the end. A beginning.

Drawn by the pull of a heartbeat I know better than my own,

I drift toward morning.

Toward warmth.

Toward my mate.

Toward our child.

Toward my future.

CHAPTER 29
THERON

The clock on the wall clicks.

Again.

And again.

And again.

The chair beneath me is cold and plastic. Smells like bleach and old sweat. I can't sit still, but I can't move either. The room is too quiet, except for the click of the damn clock, like it's mocking me.

Outside, the rain has slowed to a quiet whisper against the windows. Like the world is trying to apologize.

Like it knows what it did.

I've been sitting here for hours, or maybe it's only been minutes. And it just feels like purgatory waiting.

All I know is, she's in surgery. And she might not make it.

Rourke's beside me.

He's the only solid thing in this Goddamn world right now. Sitting next to me like a gargoyle. A silent statue guarding my fragile state.

My hands are clasped so tight between my knees I think I might break the bones.

I haven't blinked in a while.

My eyes burn.

But the tears haven't fallen.

Not yet at least.

My thoughts are seemingly empty. Blank. Like my brain's given up trying to make sense of this.

She's in surgery, being cut open, bleeding, and I'm sitting here like an ass.

Dr. Bryant said there might be a choice. That, I might lose one of them. And I said *her*.

I choose her.

I said if it comes down to it, save my mate.

I made that call.

But what if that means I lose them both?

My foot bounces. My jaw clenches. My stomach rolls. There's no part of me that feels human right now. Just a void.

Where her voice should be.

And then I hear myself say it.

Quiet, raw and broken.

Not to Rourke. Not to the nurse walking by. Not even to the God I stopped praying to years ago.

Just…out loud.

"I can't live without her."

The words land like a blow to the chest. And something inside me breaks.

"I refuse to live without her," I choke. "I can't. I won't. Rosie—"

The tears hit fast. Hot. Violent.

"My Rosie," I sob, chest heaving, "please…"

My fists press into my eyes like that'll stop it.

Like that'll undo the image of her pale on that bed, blood on her temple, her fingers still.

"I'm sorry," I whisper into my palms. "I'm so fucking sorry. I should've been there. I should've come home. I shouldn't have left."

But the words dissolve and drown. And I fall apart.

The strong Alpha who can withstand anything is gone.

All that's left is a man.

A mate on a hospital bench, waiting for the world to tell him if the love of his life survived.

My fingers dig into my hair, fists clenched so tight they shake. I can't stop the sound coming out of me. It's not a cry, it's not even human. It's something broken and raw, echoing through a waiting room that feels too white. Too sterile. Too quiet.

"I told them to save her," I rasp, chest heaving. "I told them if it came down to it, to choose her."

And I meant it.

God, I meant it.

But now the weight of that choice presses on my chest like a mountain. Because if the baby doesn't make it. If that little life we made doesn't take its first breath, she's going to look at me with those eyes.

Those soft, glassy eyes that once held every ounce of joy in the world. That lit up when she saw the ultrasound. That fluttered shut when I kissed her belly and those fears that clung to her finally let go.

And I'll see it.

The hurt. The heartbreak, and maybe even hatred.

The place where hope used to live inside her—and how empty it'll be if we lose that baby.

"She wanted this so bad," I sob, voice trembling. "For years, she prayed for this. She wished for it. Hoped."

I rock forward, elbows on my knees, hands over my face like I can hold the grief in.

"She used to cry over the negative tests. Think something was wrong with her. Said her body was broken."

My voice breaks again, sharp and small.

"And now I've given her a reason to believe it."

The tears won't stop. My throat burns. Every breath tastes like guilt.

"If we lose that baby…"

I can't finish it.

I try. My lips part. My chest heaves. But the words catch in my throat.

"She's going to hate me," I whisper, finally. "Even if she doesn't say it…she will. She'll look at me and see the man who took her choice away. Who gave her love and then ripped the future out of her hands."

The sound that escapes me isn't even a sob. It's a collapse. A body forgetting how to hold itself together

"She's going to see me and remember what we lost. Our baby. Our dream. That tiny heartbeat I didn't even get to say goodbye to."

Rourke still doesn't speak.

Doesn't move.

And I'm glad.

Because if he tries to tell me it's going to be okay, I think I'll shatter completely.

Because I don't know if it will be.

I don't know if I've already lost everything.

The doors of the waiting room swing open and Dr. Bryant steps through, still in scrubs, streaked with sweat. Her gloves are off. Her mask down. She looks like a woman who's seen the edge of something terrible and climbed back just in time.

I stand, barely able to meet her eyes.

"Rosie," I choke out. "God…tell me. Please—"

Her face is unreadable for a breath too long.

My heart punches into my throat. The world tilts. I brace my hand on the chair like I'm going to throw up.

Say it. Say it, dammit. Tell me she's alive—

"She made it."

The words hit me like sunlight through smoke.

Everything in me seizes—lungs, heart, time.

Then she says it.

A miracle in three words.

"They both did."

For a moment, I don't breathe. Can't move.

I just stand there, broken open and stitched back together in the space of a second.

Rosie.

And our baby.

Alive.

I stumble forward a step, the sob catching in my throat more animal than man. My knees buckle, but I stay upright, blinking hard against the tears that blur everything.

"They're okay?" I rasp.

Dr. Bryant nods, his voice quieter now. "She lost a lot of blood. We had to move fast. There's still a long recovery ahead. But she pulled through. They pulled through."

Somewhere, the world starts spinning again. Somewhere, the light switches back on.

"Would you like to meet your daughter?" Her smile is sweet, eager to see a reaction.

"A daughter? We have a little girl?" Silent tears fall down my face. I'm stunned. Damn near speechless.

"She's beautiful and very strong. Would you like to meet her?" She offers again, but I can't. Not without Rosie.

"No," I shake my head, and Dr. Bryant's smile fades. "Not yet, not without her mama. Rosie deserves to meet her before me. She worked too hard for me to cut her off in line." I crack a smile, tears still falling.

She glances toward the doors, her smile returning again. "They're prepping her for post-op now. You'll see her soon."

I collapse back into the chair like someone cut all my strings.

Rourke lets out a long, low breath beside me.

I close my eyes, press my hands to my face, and finally—finally—let myself believe it.

She's alive.

I didn't lose them.

Thank you. God or whatever you are. Whoever is listening. Thank you.

CHAPTER 30
ROSIE

The world comes back slowly.

Like wading up from the bottom of a lake, every part of me is heavy, waterlogged. My lashes flutter, but the light behind them is too bright. I turn my head, barely moving an inch. It feels like I've been stitched together with thread too fine to hold.

Everything hurts.

Not sharp. Just…deep. Dull. A full-body bruise that throbs with every breath.

My throat is dry. My mouth tastes like cotton. There's something tight around my middle. Something stiff in my arm. And warmth.

A hand.

Big and calloused. Wrapped tightly around mine like it's trying to keep me tethered here

Theron.

The scent hits me next. Leather. Cedar. That faint trace of salt and sweat and something wild. My Alpha.

I try to speak, but it's a cracked whisper, barely sound.

Still, he hears me.

"Rosie?"

The sound of his voice breaks something loose inside me. He's here. He's finally home.

My eyes crack open. It takes effort. But there he is, slumped forward in the chair beside my bed, eyes red, face unshaven, like he's been to hell and back. Yet still so beautiful.

"Thank God," he breathes, clutching my hand like he can't believe it's real.

I try to smile, but it's more a twitch than anything. Still, his whole-body shudders like it's the only thing he's been waiting for.

His forehead drops to our joined hands, and for a moment, I let myself float in relief.

And then, cold shock.

His forehead is still pressed to our joined hands, but when I whisper "The baby? Theron…"

He lifts his head instantly, eyes wild and shining. His voice cracks like he's been holding his breath for hours.

"They're okay, but…" Theron's voice falters, his eyes dropping to my stomach like they're too heavy to lift again.

I follow his gaze, blinking in confusion. My stomach is different. Still swollen but it's no longer the high, taut curve that had cradled our baby for months. Now it's softer, lower. Emptier.

"I don't…understand," I whisper. My hand trembles as I reach down, fingertips brushing over the tender skin. It aches, but not like before. The weight is wrong. The fullness is gone.

"Did I…?" My voice catches.

Theron nods, nears filling his eyes as he catches my hand and presses his lips to my knuckles like he's praying with them.

"Do you remember the accident?" he asks softly, the words like needles stuck in his throat. "Any of it?"

I search the broken places in my mind. I remember flashes. Pain. Screeching tires. A sharp jolt. The blare of sirens and a boy's voice. Everything else is a fog, fragments. Like trying to remember a nightmare right after waking.

"A little," I nod. "Pieces."

This thumb strokes across my hand, as if he's trying to smooth out the fractures in both of us.

"The impact causes a placental abruption," he says gently. "They… they had to perform an emergency C-section."

C-section?

"I had the baby?" My voice is so small. Broken. "But I…I don't remember."

The delivery I imagined a hundred different ways, all happened without me. The sound of their first cry. Hot tears of joy. The baby being placed on my chest. I didn't see any of it.

"Did I even hold them?" I ask, the ache in my throat unbearable. "What did they weigh? When were they born? What time? Did they cry? Are they okay?"

Each question falls from my lips like a stone, weighted with grief I know how to carry.

Theron's head bows. "I don't know," he admits, his voice coated in regret. "I wasn't allowed in, and I didn't want to meet her without you."

"Her?"

His eyes go wide with panic, lips pulling into a sheepish grimace, "Shit," he sighs. "I wasn't supposed to say that yet."

Tears fall freely now. "It's a girl?"

He nods, a blubbering sad laugh escapes him. "They told me she's beautiful. So damn small, but…strong. Just like her mama."

"Where is she?" My voice quivers, already aching with the desperate need to see her. My baby. "Can I see her?"

"She's in the NICU," he says gently, wiping tears from his eyes. "Getting all the help she needs. Breathing on her own and doing just fine. I promise, Rosie. We'll see her soon."

I close my eyes, overwhelmed. I've missed her first cry. Her first breath. Her first moment of life. But she's here. She's real.

I let out a breath I didn't know I was holding. My chest hurts with it, but I don't care. My hand tightens weakly in his.

"Are you sure?"

"I swear it," he whispers.

Tears slip down my cheeks before I can stop them. Relief. Love. Shock. All of it wrapped so tight I can't tell one from the other.

He leans closer, brushing them away with his thumb like they burn him to see.

"You scared the hell out of me, Rosie."

His voice cracks. His whole-body trembles with the weight of everything he can't say.

"I was driving…" I whisper. "I—I should've…" I remember the

sound of brakes. The scream of metal.

His thumb brushes away the thought like it's smoke.

"Stop. You came back. That's all that matters."

"You came back," I whisper.

His jaw clenches. "I never should've left."

I shake my head, "You're here now."

His breath hitches, "I almost lost you." He says it like a confession. Like a wound. "I almost lost the very reason I breathe."

His hand tightens around mine, almost painfully so, like a desperate attempt to keep me forever in his grasp.

"Rosie…" His voice breaks. "I can't ever lose you. I can't."

He leans forward, pressing his forehead to mine, and when he speaks again, it's barely a whisper, like the words cost him everything to say.

"I love you. I love you so much it almost killed me today."

Every syllable. Every ounce of that pain and devotion. It threads through his fingers and into mine, settles in my bones like a second heartbeat.

I close my eyes, fresh tears sliding into my hairline.

I lift our joined hands with what little strength I have and press a kiss to his knuckles, my lips trembling.

"Shh," I whisper, brushing my thumb over the back of his hand. "We're okay."

His eyes squeeze shut.

"All three of us," I breathe. "We're okay, Theron. We're still here."

He lets out a sound—part wail, part relief—and leans down, burying his face against the side of my neck like he can't hold himself up any longer.

And I just hold him there. Letting him cry. Letting him be vulnerable and broken in the safety of my love.

He pulls back, just enough to look at me. His eyes are red, wet, feral with love and fear and something that's only ever belonged to me.

His hand rises, shaking as it cups my cheek, thumb ghosting over the tender skin beneath my eye. He's looking at me like he still doesn't believe I'm real. Like I'll vanish if he blinks too long.

"Rosie," he breathes, voice raw. "My Rosie."

Then he kisses me.

Slow.

Reverent.

A kiss that isn't about hunger or passion, but feel like home. About everything we almost lost. Everything we still have. Everything we'll build, together.

It's a kiss that promises a love deeper than other. A life shared with trial and tribulations. A bond that runs deeper than the mark made years ago.

"I love you," he whispers.

CHAPTER 31
THERON
3 YEARS LATER

Our daughter's laughter rings through the hallway like windchimes in spring. Full of that untouchable kind of joy only toddlers seem to know.

Robin.

That's what we named her.

Our little bird who loves to play and laugh and snuggle tight with her mama when she crash lands.

She's barefoot, running with a stuffed fox clutched in one hand and a spatula in the other, her riot of curls bouncing behind her like a celebration. Her giggles echo off the walls, infecting you with a warmth that makes you believe everything in the world is good after all.

Somewhere behind her, Rosie laughs too. It's the bright, unfiltered laugh that I fell in love with. She's slower than our girl, waddling after her with mock-exasperation and an unmistakable glow in her eyes. Her belly rounds out in front of her, full and firm with baby number two, and when she catches my eye from down the hall, her smile is radiant enough to level me.

This is the life.

The one I dreamed of. The messy, chaotic, beautiful life I thought I would miss because of an accident. But now it's mine.

The house is still a work in progress. Some rooms half-finished, tools tucked behind doors, paint swatches tapped to corners we swore we'd repaint last year. But somehow, even the mess feels like home. Like love in motion. We've lived here almost three years, and yet there's still so much to do.

It's hard to finish renovations with a toddler who insists her stuffed animals need tea parties mid-paint job or begs me to dance with her in the middle of hammering baseboards. And honestly, I wouldn't trade it.

The nursery was the first room we completed, fresh walls, soft lighting, new carpet, all finished in the dead of night and with only kisses from my mate to keep me going.

I didn't get to build the cradle like I swore I would. Time was stolen a little too quickly from us. We were still in the middle of purchasing the house when our little girl came early. But I will build one for this next baby. I've already started drafting the plans. Oak varnished with little hand-carved foxes at each corner.

Sometimes, when the house quiets down for the night. When Robin is tucked into her bed, and Rosie's asleep with one hand on her belly, I think about that first birth.

Our daughter was pulled from her belly while Rosie lay unconscious, because of a damn accident. I remember sitting out in the lobby, feeling like a ghost, listening to the white noise of a busy hospital while my mind spiraled into an abyss.

I feel a little ashamed when I think back on it. I had refused to see the baby before Rosie could. It feels a little like I was rejecting her, and I hate to think that it might be a little true.

At the time it just felt like I had to wait in line. I didn't deserve to see her first. I hadn't suffered like Rosie had.

So I waited my turn, and I'm grateful I did.

Because when she finally held our tiny, sweet baby girl...God. I'm far from being articulate enough to even describe it.

Rosie cried and cried, a wide smile on her face, whispering words of love that only a true mother could express. It was the most beautiful thing I had ever seen.

And I was grateful. So fucking grateful.

That single moment changed my life forever.

I grin, watching Robin as she tears through the kitchen and crashes directly into my legs with a giggle.

"Daddy!" she chirps.

"Hey, angel," I chuckle, scooping her up.

She's got her mother's spirit. That radiant sweetness that charms everyone she meets. But her face? Her eyes? That little stubborn tilt of her chin?

All me.

Rosie catches up a few seconds later, flushed and beautiful in a way that knocks the air right out of my lungs. Her maternity dress hugs her bump, her hands bracing her back, tired from being on her feet all damn day.

"Caught your girl again," I say, bouncing our daughter against my hip.

Rosie leans up for a kiss, eyes wrinkling in the corners. "She's too fast for me. Must've inherited that from her father."

"Damn right she did."

Our little one reaches for Rosie's belly next, murmuring "baby" and giving it a proud little pat. Rosie's eyes go soft.

"Not long now," she whispers.

We're not finding out the gender again—just like last time. Rosie says it's more fun that way and I can't deny. It makes the wait just that little bit more exciting.

The second baby's due any day now. And I swear, even though I try—I really do—I can't stop wanting her.

Every night, I tell myself to let her rest. And every night, I lose that battle.

She'll smile at me just once, touch my hand under the dinner table, tilt her head a little and suddenly I'm on my knees, thanking God I get to worship her.

She lets me. Every time. Moaning softly, cradling her belly, whispering my name like a promise as I tell her how fucking gorgeous she is. How perfect. How I'll never stop loving her. Or filling her. Or making her mine over and over again.

Yeah, I lost that battle. And I'll keep losing it. Gladly.

She chuckles now, clearly reading my thoughts. Her hand comes up to rest against my chest, fingers brushing my collarbone. "You're staring again."

"I always stare," I admit. "I'm in love."

She blushes.

"You are trouble, sir," she teases. "One more baby and we'll run out of room."

"We'll build an addition," I grin. "Or move again."

Rosie laughs like I'm joking. I'm not.

I'd build her a palace if she asked. I'd build her a castle made of books. And I'd name every tower after our babies.

There was a time we weren't sure this would ever happen. A time of tests and tears and rooms turned into libraries just to cope with the emptiness. Now? That same hope that once broke us has bloomed into something loud and wild and soft. Something with a giggle and sticky fingers.

Rosie's hand rests on my chest, and I can feel the exhaustion starting to pull at her, telling her body it's time to rest.

Robin squirms between us, still clutching her spatula like a sword. And just like her mama, she too is fighting to need to sleep.

Rosie smooths a hand over our daughter's wild curls. "Alright, little bird," she murmurs. "Time to roost."

Robin pouts. "Noooo, Mama. Play!"

"You can play in your dreams," Rosie says gently, brushing a kiss to her cheek. "The best adventures happen there."

She reaches out, and Robin curls into her without protest, head dropping onto Rosie's shoulder, those sweet dark lashes already beginning to flutter.

I follow them down the hall as Rosie carries her into the nursery.

She hums as she rocks her in a slow repetitive motion, all while singing a lullaby under her breath, lulling our little bird for bed.

She's so beautiful like this.

Hair loose. Dress clinging to her bump. One hand cradling Robin's head as she settles her into the bed, the other stroking her back in soothing circles.

I wait just outside the door, arms folded, watching through the cracked frame as she tucks our daughter in. She leans down and whispers something sweet and coated in motherly love and Robin sighs, shifting into her blanket nest like she belongs to the stars.

Rosie turns.

And I'm there.

Waiting.

Wanting.

The moment the nursery door clicks shut, I press her gently against the hallway wall, my hands braced on either side of her head, caging her in with everything I feel.

Her breath catches. Her eyes flick up, catching the heat in mine. She knows.

She always knows.

She tilts her head, that sleepy, knowing smile playing on her lips. "Bedtime's not just for her, you know," she whispers.

My voice is already ruined. "Oh, I'm not tired."

She starts to laugh, but it dies in her throat when I lean in and kiss her.

Heated and possessive.

She melts against me, soft hands sliding under my shirt, the curve of her belly pressing into me like gravity itself wants us fused together.

I growl. The sound slipping between her parted lips as my mouth moves against hers. My hand finds the side of her throat, thumb dragging along the delicate line of her jaw.

"You're mine now, mama," I whisper against her mouth. "No more running."

She gasps—her body already reacting to the promise under my skin—and I feel her shift in my arms. So responsive. So needy.

Just like me.

I just can't help it.

I've been watching her all damn day. Watching her glow, watching her move, watching her smile like she isn't driving me insane just existing.

I scoop her up, bridal-style, my grip just a little too tight. My fingers press into her thigh, my arm snug around her back as I stride toward our room like a beast on a leash.

Only there's no leash anymore.

Because once the door closes—

I'm going to devour her.

Because she's mine.

My home, my fire, my future.

And God help me, but I'll never stop needing her.

EPILOGUE
ROSIE

The house is finally quiet.

Both babies are asleep. The real kind of sleep, not that fake nap-trap that fools you into relaxing before the next wail. The monitor is silent. The dishes are done. My body aches in places I didn't know even existed before motherhood, and yet, I couldn't be more at peace.

I shift beneath the covers and turn a page in my book. It's almost ten. Once upon a time, I thought that was an early bedtime. Now? It's practically reckless.

Phoenix is almost one. My little boy with wild dark curls and a stubborn attitude, always babbling, always climbing, always testing limits with that mischievous grin. And Robin, our bold, beautiful firstborn, is the boss of the whole house. She's got her daddy wrapped around her tiny finger so tight, I genuinely worry how he's going to handle it when she starts elementary school next year.

Yesterday, Theron came home late from work. He just missed bedtime. He sulked about it for hours and then insisted that tonight's bedtime duties were all his. That also means he's on call for any middle-of-the-night wakeups. Which is why he isn't in bed beside me right now.

I loved this Alpha before we had children. But now? Now I've seen him cuddle a sick toddler at three am., sing lullabies with a voice that could kill a deer and carry car seats like they're made of porcelain. And I swear to God, there is nothing sexier than a man who dotes on his babies.

I hear a soft creak of the nursery door down the hall. His heavy footsteps pad toward our bedroom. I don't look up right away. I wait, savoring the anticipation like dessert.

Theron appears in the doorway, shirtless, sweatpants hanging low on his hips. His hair is damp from a shower. Jaw freshly shaved.

"Robin is out once more." He says sleepily. Stumbling into the room and collapsing face-first beside me.

"Nightmare?" I bookmark my page and set my book on the nightstand.

"She said daddy wouldn't look at her." He lifts his head, eyes soft and guilt stricken.

It hits him hard, every time. He has some remorse for choices made at her birth and him being away for work every so often doesn't make it any easier.

"She just missed you," I say gently, petting his head. "She'll be just fine."

He hums, leaning into my touch. Seeking comfort, at least that's what I thought until his brows furrow.

"Your scent," he murmurs. "It's different."

The hair on the back of my neck stands on end.

Good. He noticed.

"Dr. Bryant did warn my heat would be returning soon." I say feigning ignorance.

He lifts his head a little higher. "Yeah?"

I nod, shifting against the pillows. "Might have to send the kids off for a few days."

He grins, crawling closer. "Your mom's or mine?"

"Wanna flip a coin?"

I pull the blanket back, revealing the thin cotton nightgown I'm wearing. It's soft and old and just sheer enough to leave little to the imagination.

"Rosie." He growls, a warning.

"Mmm?"

"I've been on edge all day. And now you're telling me your body's about to go into heat?"

"Not yet," I tease, tracing his jaw with one finger. "But soon."

His mouth finds my shoulder, teeth scraping gently. "You trying to kill me, baby?"

I arch into him, breath catching as his hand slides under my gown, warm fingers trailing up my thigh.

"Not kill you," I whisper, smiling. "Just give you a warm-up."

His grip tightens, groaning into my skin.

"It's been a few weeks," I murmur, playful and breathless. "You sure you're up for this?"

He chuckles darkly, "You know damn well I am."

"Good." I hook my leg around his hip. "Because I want you Alpha. Now."

The second those words leave my lips, something snaps within him.

He growls, and surges forward, mouth crashing into mine like he's trying to consume me. His hands grip my thighs, rough and possessive, dragging me down the bed like prey. The mattress shifts beneath us, sheets twisting and tangling.

"Fuck, Rosie," he snarls against my lips. "I've missed you."

I gasp as he yanks my nightgown up to my hips, revealing exactly what I wanted him to find.

As a parent I've learned how to cut some corners to save time. Like not wearing panties when wanting to get fucked.

"God, you really are trying to kill me." He practically drools as he stares at my bare pussy.

"And you're wasting time," I counter, smirking. "One whimper from those kids and this whole thing's over."

His eyes flash, hungry and wild.

"Fair point," he smirks. "Get on your knees."

I move fast, bending forward, ass high, hands braced against the pillows, heat pulsing between my thighs. I feel him behind me, feel the weight of him shift as he takes his position.

Then he grabs my hips and slams into me.

One brutal, perfect thrust that steals the air from my lungs.

"Theron!" I choke out, voice breaking, head dropping as he fills me deep, stretching me open until I swear I can feel him in my womb.

His pace is relentless from the start. No buildup. No hesitation. Just pure, primal fucking.

I bite my lip, trying to keep quiet. But the sound of skin against skin, the obscene wet slap of his cock inside me, makes it impossible. A moan, far too loud for this *secret operation*, slips out.

"Shh, sweetheart," he pants, leaning over me, hand sliding around to cover my mouth. "Don't end our fun too soon."

His palm muffles the next cry as he drives deeper and harder.

Each thrust punches deep, hitting my cervix with a force that should knock the breath from me. But all it does is make me crave more. This. This is what I needed. What I'd been aching for while he was gone.

Wild. Feral. Unapologetic.

The kind of fucking that leaves bruises on your soul. That carves his name into every inch of me.

I moan against his palm, the sound muffled but desperate. More, more, more. And he hears every word I can't say.

"I know, Rosie," he growls against my shoulder. "I know, baby. I'll give you exactly what you need."

He leans forward, his massive body covering mine, chest pressed to my back, sweat-slicked skin dragging across mine like velvet and fire. His hips don't stop. They grind harder, deeper.

Then, his teeth.

He sinks them into the mark on my neck, clamping down, anchoring me to him in the most primal way. The pain is sharp and delicious, a lightning bolt through my spine, and I scream behind his hand.

That's when I feel it, his knot. Swelling inside me, hot and thick and demanding.

The pressure builds until I can barely breathe.

And when it catches, when it locks us together, every breath leaves my body. My mouth falls open, only a shattered whimper escaping as white-hot pleasure detonates through me.

Theron grunts against my skin, still biting down, his body trembling with the force of his own release. Thick ropes of come ejaculate into me, flooding my womb, every pulse of his cock met with the rhythmic clenching of my walls.

I'm shaking. Sweating. Split wide and filled so deep, it's a wet dream come true.

Our breathing slows. The haze lifts and Theron shifts us gently. Guiding us to lay on our sides, still joined, his knot firmly lodged inside me. One arm wraps around my middle, the other curls beneath my head, holding me tight, his chest warm against my spine.

I sigh, utterly spent, eyes fluttering shut.

And just as sleep dares to find us after our escapades.

A baby cries.

We both groan in unison.

"I got it," Theron murmurs, pressing a kiss to my temple and shifting just slightly, as far as the tie allows at least.

"No, you're stuck, Alpha." I mutter, a sleepy, remorseful smile tugging at my lips.

Theron groans, "How do we…do this?" he asks, looking more bewildered than ever. The concern on his face is genuine, but so is the ridiculousness of our situation.

"Slowly," I whisper, nudging his leg with mine. "That's how."

The next ten minutes are a mix of awkward shuffling, muffled curses, breathless giggles, and failed escape attempts. We try different angles, positions, and prayers. Every movement is a delicate dance of

"Ow. Wait! Okay now pull," and "Stop laughing, you're making it worse."

At one point, he moans—actually moans—and I slap his arm with a scolding glare. "Don't you dare get hard again. I will kill you."

He grins, unapologetic. "I'm trying not to but you're…ugh, everything hurts and you're so soft."

"Shut up, horndog."

Eventually, finally, we manage to untie. It's not pretty. There's some sliding. Some unnecessary squelching. But freedom is won.

Theron immediately bolts out of bed, pulling up a pair of sweats while muttering something about our child and parental responsibility.

When he comes back, he's grinning like an idiot.

"What?" I ask, suspicious.

He tries, and fails, to keep a straight face. "She thought she heard mama in pain."

My face goes scarlet.

"Oh my God," I groan, dragging the blanket over my head. "Please tell me you played it off."

"I told her it was a bad dream," he says, chest puffed with pride. "And that daddy would never let anything hurt her mama."

"Don't gloat. It was the heat, not you." I peek behind the blanket.

"Liar." He chuckles, climbing back into bed beside me, pulling me into his arms.

We lay there, tangled up in love and exhaustion, already knowing we'll laugh about this again someday.

9 7 9 8 2 1 8 8 7 0 1 2 6